IN THE SHADOW
OF THE BEAR

IN THE SHADOW OF THE BEAR

JUDITH ST. GEORGE

G. P. PUTNAM'S SONS
NEW YORK

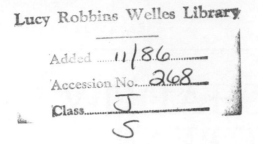
Copyright © 1983 by Judith St. George
All rights reserved. Published simultaneously in
Canada by General Publishing Co. Limited, Toronto.
Printed in the United States of America
First Impression
Book design by Nanette Stevenson

Library of Congress Cataloging in Publication Data
St. George, Judith.
In the shadow of the bear.
Summary: Seventeen-year-old Annie's week in Alaska
at her father's company's camp stretches her mental and
physical limits as she must deal with hostile Russians
and survival in the wilderness.
[1. Alaska—Fiction] I. Title.
PZ7.S142In 1983   [Fic]   83-17607
ISBN 0-399-21015-6

To *James* and *Philip*,
without whose help this story
couldn't have been told

1

The hotel walls were so thin all the noise and smells from Dad's room next door curled into Annie's room; the cigar smoke, the clink of a bottle against glasses, laughter, voices. Most of all, the voices. Every time Annie drifted off to sleep, a guffaw or a burst of male banter would wake her. At last she gave up and turned on her light to read the paperback she had bought earlier.

At first the men next door had talked business, the latest price of lead and zinc, problems out at Little Salmon Camp, who in the company had been moved up and who had been laid off, and Annie had been able to read through that. But then, as the smoke had thickened and voices were raised, the men had started in on politics and about the president's upcoming trip to Geneva to sign a nuclear disarmament treaty with the Russians, and Annie hadn't been able to read through that. Some of the men insisted that there was no way the Commies could be trusted, treaty or no treaty, that up here in Alaska, where the Russian mainland wasn't even sixty miles away, they were especially vulnerable to the Soviet bear. The rest of the men, Dad included, argued that they'd never know if a treaty could work unless they tried it.

The louder and more vehement the discussion grew, the more wide awake Annie became. Although Annie's older sister Elizabeth and brother Scott were active in anti-nuclear groups, Annie had never gotten involved. It wasn't that she wasn't interested; she was. She read all their pamphlets and literature and knew from a Social Studies film what would happen if a one-megaton bomb were dropped over New York. But Elizabeth and Scott had nagged and pressured her so much, she had backed off. She knew that with any project they were in charge of, she'd just end up being their tag-along kid sister. As usual.

Then, a year ago, a U.S. and Soviet Union moratorium on nuclear arms production and stockpiling had been announced, to be followed by a nuclear disarmament treaty, and Annie's, and everyone else's hopes, had been raised. The treaty would work. It *had* to work.

Still the argument next door continued, the talk now edged with anger. Then Dad's voice rose above the others.

"Hey, let's call it a night. Annie's in the next room trying to sleep, and she's got a big day tomorrow."

"How long are you and Annie gonna be out at camp, Frank?" someone asked.

Dad hesitated. Annie could picture him taking a drag on his cigar before answering. The only time Dad smoked cigars or drank whiskey was when he was with his old wilderness buddies from his days as a young geologist up here in Alaska. Now he was a big executive and only came to Alaska in the summer to check out the company's exploration camps.

"I don't know. Five days, maybe a week. When Elizabeth and Scott were seventeen and went out to Little Salmon Camp, I could hardly drag them away after ten days."

There was a murmur of voices in reply, comments and more laughter as the men called their good nights and left. Annie squeezed her eyes shut and shivery red lines danced in a

8

panicky cadence across her vision. I'm not Elizabeth or Scott, she thought. I'm Ann Jamison Sloane and I don't even want to be up here in Alaska. And I especially don't want to go out to camp. A week. Dad hadn't said anything about staying a whole week.

Annie picked up her paperback again. Not that she was interested in it, but she was wide awake now and even though her curtains were drawn and it was past eleven o'clock, here above the Arctic Circle in Kotzebue, the summer sun still hadn't completely set. After their long trip from California, Annie should have been tired, especially since they'd passed through three time zones and in the process lost three hours of sleep, but she wasn't. Her seventeenth summer was here and her trip out to Little Salmon Camp was heavy on her mind.

2

It was hard to read in the airplane, but Annie was determined to stick with it. That way she wouldn't have to look down at the miles and miles of open tundra that had been unrolling endlessly beneath their plane ever since she and her father had taken off from the Kotzebue airport and headed north toward Little Salmon Camp. Luckily, Dad was too busy flying to bother with his usual sightseeing lectures. Although Dad had earned his pilot's license years ago, he was really into the experience of flying the new company Cessna.

The trouble was, the flight was bumpy and Annie, who had forgotten to take anything for motion sickness this morning, could already taste the greasy hash she'd had for lunch edging up toward the back of her throat. She closed her paperback, leaned her head back and glanced out the window. They were flying over low limestone mountains now, gray, rounded, bald mountains that rose from the flat plains as if a pump had inflated big bubbles on the level landscape. At least the mountains weren't overwhelming like the peaks of the Brooks Range in the distance, abrupt, jagged, and shouldered with snow, even now in the middle of August. As soon as they were over the mountains, the tundra resumed, crisscrossed with braided streams and twisting rivers, and dotted with looking-glass ponds.

"Look, Annie, a moose." Dad sounded as excited as a kid, although over the years Annie figured he had probably seen more moose than he could count.

Nevertheless, Annie obediently turned in the direction where her father was pointing. Sure enough, a huge moose, ungainly on thin clothespin legs, stood ankle deep in a tundra pond feeding. At the sound of the plane circling overhead, he raised his head, revealing a rack of wide antlers that seemed topheavy enough to tip him over.

Dad reached over and squeezed Annie's knee. "They don't grow moose like that in California," he joked as he maneuvered the Cessna lower.

Annie's stomach heaved. "Dad, please don't circle any more."

For the first time, Dad noticed Annie's pale face and teary eyes and he grimaced. "Sorry about that, Babes. I forgot about your shaky stomach. I used to get airsick when I first started working in the field too. You'll grow out of it."

It was easier to nod agreement than to argue. At seventeen, it was getting a little late for Annie to be growing out of anything, as well as growing in any other direction, like taller or bigger or stronger the way she had counted on doing all her life so she would fit in with the rest of the family, giants all.

Annie sighed and glanced at the plastic bag stuck in the pocket of the plane door. If she took it out and opened it, she was sure to get sick. No, by pretending it wasn't there, maybe she could keep everything down.

"How much farther, Dad?"

"Only another thirty miles or so. See, there's Niyuk straight ahead and Little Salmon Camp is about twenty-five miles

11

beyond that. I'm taking us out of the way so you can see Niyuk. It's a small Eskimo settlement on the Niyuk River."

Niyuk was small, just a scattering of shacks haphazardly thrown together on the banks of a river that from this altitude looked like a length of bright blue twisted yarn. Toy-size people moved among the shacks, a few of them looking up and waving as the plane passed over.

"Their shacks have to be built on stilts," Dad explained. "This far north above the Arctic Circle, there's only a couple of feet of soil covering hundreds, sometimes thousands, of feet of permanently frozen earth. Building on the permafrost would thaw it, and then the melted ground would heave. That's why it's called barren ground. No trees or plants with any kind of root system can grow in the tundra, and besides, the growing season is much too short."

It was beginning to sound like a seminar. Dad was so full of information, it was fatal ever to ask him a question unless you wanted more information than you could possibly assimilate. Annie nodded and rested her head back against her seat again. "That's amazing," she commented.

How long Dad discussed permafrost, Annie had no idea, but all of a sudden, she realized he had changed the subject and was talking about her. And college. ". . . so your grades probably aren't strong enough to apply for early acceptance like Elizabeth and Scott did."

But Annie wasn't interested in acceptance, early or any other kind. She didn't even want to go to college. She wanted to work full-time at the Walther Art Center where she'd had a summer job these past two years. Still, there was no way she was going to tell Dad that. He'd rant and rave until she promised to apply. No, for the time being, she'd keep quiet.

With Annie's college situation taken care of, Dad moved on. "I wonder how Elizabeth is making out," he said. "I'm sure Scott is doing okay, but Elizabeth will have her hands full."

12

Elizabeth at twenty-two was assistant director this summer at a Wilderness Survival Camp on the Colorado River, responsible for fifty twelve-year-olds. Scott, just twenty, was playing soccer for a professional team. There was no doubt in Annie's mind that they were both doing fine, like they always had. Mom, who was head surgical nurse at St. Martin's Hospital, would be fine too. It was herself that Annie was worried about. Could she really be traveling by plane to live in a mineral exploration camp 150 miles north of the Arctic Circle for a week? It didn't seem possible.

For years Annie had been dreading this, her seventeenth summer, when it would be her turn to come to Alaska with Dad the way Elizabeth and Scott had when they were seventeen. Now the time was here and Annie was on her way to the End of the World when she would much rather be back home with her friend Lisa, settling down by the pool for the afternoon with their Sony Walkmans. But instead of a bathing suit, she was bundled up in a sweater, a down parka, wool socks and high rubber Extratuf boots that she'd had to buy in the hated children's department because her feet were so small.

Dad was still talking, reminiscing now about the years he had spent in Alaska when it was *real* wilderness. As Annie smiled and nodded as if she were listening, she noticed something down on the ground out of the corner of her eye, something moving in the treeless plains. It was a bear and two cubs running away from the roar of their Cessna. The mother shone almost silver in the flat light and her fur rippled over her powerful back. Despite her size, she ran effortlessly, swatting first one cub on the rear and then the other as she tried to keep them going. The cubs were small and dark, almost black.

Now Dad saw the bears too. "Wow, look at the grizzlies," he exclaimed, flying in lower for a better look. "You can't see it from here, but there's a hump behind the sow's head. You can't ever mistake a barren ground grizzly for anything else. And those first-year cubs with her only weighed a pound when they were born last winter. They'll stay with her until their third summer when they're fully grown, and you'd better believe that she'll defend them with her life. Isn't she magnificent?"

"Yes."

Annie wasn't even aware of answering. Grizzly bears. At some time she must have heard talk of bears, but it hadn't really registered. Now it was registering loud and clear. They were in grizzly bear country. It was beyond her wildest imaginings. Hypnotized by the sight of the three bears eating up the ground with their flying feet, Annie stared. The sow was more than magnificent. She was all-mighty. Bigger than life. Terrifying.

Without warning, the plane hit an air pocket and dropped twenty feet. It was too much. Everything that had been poised at the back of Annie's throat came up with a rush. Quickly she grabbed for the plastic bag and opened it just in time.

3

They didn't have that much farther to go. "Just hang in there a few more minutes, Annie," Dad urged. "The Little Salmon radio is out. I'll have to buzz camp to let them know we've arrived so they can send their helicopter over for us."

Annie lay back in her seat, not even trying to figure out what a helicopter had to do with anything as they flew in low over the camp, a little huddle of tents and shacks in the vastness that was the Arctic tundra. A couple of men stood in the clearing and waved as Dad circled, dipped his wings and headed away from camp over a series of rolling mountains toward the landing strip.

Annie felt the pressure of the flaps lowering as the motor slowed. But they were still in the middle of the limestone mountains that her father called talus slopes, with no possible place to land. Nevertheless, Dad was all concentration as he pushed the stick forward. Annie sucked in her breath as she realized that mountains or no mountains, they were about to come down.

There, right beneath them, was a narrow strip of gravel tucked in between the talus slopes. Dad made two sweeping turns to the left and came in low, his wheels slapping down hard, then shuddering as they bounced along the gravel bed. But they were headed straight into a mountain!

Annie couldn't yell or cry out or even cover her face the way she did in horror movies as the plane jounced over the rough ground with the mountain looming larger and larger ahead of them. All of a sudden, Dad hit the brakes hard and made an abrupt right-angle turn that slammed Annie hard into her seat belt. Now they were headed away from the mountain, splattering through shallow puddles as they taxied to a stop.

Dad let out a sigh. "I always forget what a tight landing this is. I swear it's the only airstrip in the world that makes a dogleg turn to avoid hitting a mountain." And then he laughed.

Laughed! Annie's hands were clammy wet and her stomach was lodged somewhere up in her chest as her father made a few last-minute adjustments and unbuckled his seat belt. Suddenly her stomach gave a warning lurch. In seconds, she was free of her seat belt, out of the plane and racing across the gravel strip. As she leaned over, surprised there was anything left to be sick with, she felt Dad's reassuring arm around her shoulders and his handkerchief pressed into her hand.

"I forgot my Bonamine," Annie apologized. Her face was splotchy red and a little drip she didn't know was there balanced on the end of her nose.

"I'm really sorry, Babes. It's a bumpy trip and this landing strip leaves a whole lot to be desired." Dad massaged Annie's back. "At least they'll have a new one next year. They've been blasting all summer."

As Annie wiped her face with the handkerchief and blew her nose, she decided that next year didn't much interest her. She handed back Dad's handkerchief and drew in deep lungfuls of air. The damp coldness of it helped and although she knew that walking around would help too, there was no time for that. The persistent thump, thump, thump racketing in her head had materialized into a blue-and-white helicopter that was swooping down toward them in a blast of wind and noise. Absurdly, *Olyve Oil* was painted on one side.

Annie shivered, and she wasn't sure if that was from the cold or from the thought of climbing into such a fragile blue grasshopper. Now the wind from the blades was blowing her thick brown hair into a tangled bush as the helicopter settled down neatly behind the Cessna. The helicopter door opened and the pilot waved them over.

Once inside the helicopter, a roar like a chain saw filled the cockpit. "Lester, this is my daughter, Annie. Annie, meet Lester, the best bush copter pilot in Alaska." Dad shouted the introductions.

Lester shifted a big wad of chewing tobacco from one side of his mouth to the other and muttered something that sounded like "Howdy." With a full beard and mustache as well as big mirror reflecting dark glasses shielding his eyes, it was impossible to tell what he looked like, let alone what he was thinking. What he seemed, mostly, was bored. Annie hoped he was bored. If only he hadn't seen her get sick. And if only she could make it to camp without getting sick again. She ran her tongue around her cottony mouth and swallowed past the bitter rawness of her throat.

Almost immediately they were flying low over the bald gray mountains that separated Little Salmon Camp from the landing strip. Determined not to humiliate herself again, Annie clamped her mouth tight and stared straight ahead at the casual cluster of tents and shacks that spilled along the banks of a river. The Lanatak River was a rushing, clear blue stream bordered by the usual alder and willow growth that seemed to flourish in the tundra wherever there was water. Gravel paths sectioned off camp like the markers of a child's board game, with the players, the Little Salmon crew, waiting on their squares.

17

The deafening clatter of the rotor blades persisted as the horizontal motion of the helicopter abruptly changed to vertical. They were landing. Annie clutched her seat with both hands for the jarring impact, but the skids touched down as gently as a leaf falling and the terrible racket ceased. Dad was out of the helicopter first, with one hand holding onto his hat and the other stretched out in greeting to a big man who rushed toward him. The man, who boasted a full red beard, was almost totally bald. He and Dad gave each other a bear hug and a couple of slaps on the back, laughing and both talking at once. Annie sighed and climbed out herself, wishing she could rinse her mouth and brush her teeth before she had to meet anyone. But her father was already walking toward her with the tall man in tow. Two other men stood farther back, as if not to interfere with the reunion.

"Annie, this is George MacNair, an old classmate of mine from the College of Mines, though as you can see by his hairline, he's a good deal older. Big Mac is Project Geologist here at Little Salmon. Mac, this is Annie, our baby, here for her toughening-up summer." Dad laughed, but Annie realized with a jolt that he wasn't kidding. Although it had never been mentioned, Annie knew with sudden clarity that toughening her up was exactly what her father hoped to accomplish.

Sometimes Annie wondered if she really was a Sloane. If it weren't for her thick, too-curly hair just like her mother's, and the cleft in her chin that was identical to her father's, with the same gray-green eyes as Elizabeth's and Dad's, she would have been certain she was just a stray they had picked up somewhere. As it was, she had never been able to keep up with the rest of them, the skiers, campers, backpackers, athletes, that were her parents and siblings.

Before she was twelve, Annie had broken her collarbone falling off a jungle gym, broken her leg skiing, and had five stitches in her forehead from being hit by a bat in a softball game. At that point, as far as Annie was concerned, her athletic career, which had never really begun, was over, and since then, she had become adept at appearing to enter into all the family outings while actually staying very much on the sidelines.

Mac took a stub of a cigar from his mouth and stuck out his hand. Annie shook it, her small hand disappearing into what looked like a baseball mitt. "Hi," she said, trying not to breathe his way and not sure whether to call him Mr. Mac-Nair, George, or Mac.

"Howdy, Annie, it's good to meet you. So you're the last of Frank's kids. I've put Elizabeth and Scott through their paces, so I guess I can put you through yours." Mac grinned, revealing a gold front tooth that shone brightly in a mouthful of big, horsey teeth. "You'll have a great time here at Little Salmon out in the field, I guarantee."

What did out in the field mean? Puzzled, Annie glanced at her father, but he was busy looking for something in his jacket pocket and didn't meet her eye.

"You'll be running rod for Robert." Mac had a surprisingly soft and musical voice for such a big man. "We're real short-handed so you'll be a big help as Robert's rod man. Sorry, Robert's rod person. I gotta keep up with the times, right, Frank?" Mac nudged Dad to make sure he got the joke.

"Dad?" Annie's voice wasn't very forceful, but she knew her father heard because he glanced up. And when she saw his sheepish expression, she knew it was bad news. It was the same expression he had worn the day Mom had found out he had taken up hang gliding without discussing it with her first.

Now he put his arm around Annie and smiled down at her. She always felt ridiculous when he did that because he was so tall and she was so short. Both Dad and Scott were over six feet tall, with Mom at five feet eight and Elizabeth at five feet ten. Annie barely reached five feet, and weighed in at one hundred pounds. The Runt of the Litter. Annie hated that expression and hated the way she always had to laugh when someone called her that as if she had never heard it before.

She struggled out from under her father's arm. "Dad?"

"You'll have a great time, just like Mac says. You'll go out in the field by helicopter every day to help with the survey work. You'll be well paid and have a wonderful experience. You certainly don't want to just sit around camp all week, do you?" Dad ran his words together, as if to get the discussion over with.

Annie couldn't believe that Dad had arranged this without telling her. That was stupid. Of course she could. It was just the sort of thing he would arrange. There was a prolonged moment of awkward silence, broken only by the sound of the rushing river beyond camp, the background drone of the generator, and two huge ravens on the riverbank squabbling over a dead salmon.

Mac tried to ease the tension. "Robert's a capable party chief and you don't have to worry about the grizzlies. You're much too small for them to bother with."

Mac laughed, so Annie had to assume he was kidding. But the shudder that started at the base of her spine and shivered up her back was proof enough that, as far as she was concerned, it was no joking matter.

4

Little Salmon Camp had suffered its share of problems during the summer and Mac and Dad got right down to hashing them over. The radio, which was out of commission, needed to be flown back to Kotzebue for repairs, and the pump for pumping water into camp from the Lanatak River had been malfunctioning on and off since June. With the basic surveying and drilling completed, Little Salmon was pared down to a minimum crew that was finishing up some last-minute survey work. From a crew of sixty with three helicopters, sixteen drillers and three cooks, Little Salmon was down to Mac, four surveyors, a helicopter mechanic, Lester and one cook. And now Dad and Annie.

Annie didn't care how many people were left in camp. The only thing that mattered was that she had to go out in the field. It was inevitable, she knew. When Dad's jaw got that set look, there was no point arguing, especially since Mac said having her work would release a man needed around camp, although how she could be of use to anyone in the field was beyond her.

As her father and Mac discussed Little Salmon's problems, Annie shifted from one foot to another, idly glancing around.

21

There were twenty-five or thirty tents grouped together only fifty yards or so from the Lanatak River that noisily burbled and splashed over smooth rounded rocks. A bald gray limestone mountain rose abruptly behind camp, with pockets of snow dotting its recesses. On the other side of the river, a single file of caribou paraded across a low ridge, their antlers a dramatic silhouette against the leaden sky. The two ravens fighting over the dead fish had been joined by three or four more and the racket the huge birds set up was fierce. Annie shivered as a cold wind out of the north cut into her parka and swirled scraps of paper and fine dust in frantic circles. A week here at dreary, treeless, gray End of the World stretched ahead like an eternity.

Suddenly Annie realized she had to go to the bathroom. Maybe it was the sound of the gurgling water that did it, but from a minor annoyance, she was confronted with a full-blown emergency.

". . . burned more drill bits than any driller I ever had," Mac was saying.

Annie nudged her father and when he looked down, she whispered, "Where's the john?"

Mac didn't give him a chance to answer. "Farthest shed over, Annie. It's your basic outhouse. Throw some lime in when you're finished. It's known as the Arctic flush." And both he and Dad laughed.

Basic was right. The outhouse consisted of a board with two holes suspended over steel oil drums with a box of lime and a shovel in the corner. When Annie was finished, she peered around the corner of the outhouse. Dad and Mac were headed into the office shack, a big nylon shell that looked more permanent than the other tents. She'd have to poke around on her own until she found a place to wash up. Although Dad had bragged that Little Salmon was one of the better equipped exploration camps in Alaska, from what Annie had seen so far, it could be that the Lanatak River was their basic Arctic washroom.

So when she found the bathhouse, it was a pleasant surprise. It was complete with two sinks, two showers, and running hot water, the find of the day. After Annie had washed up, brushed her tousled snarl of hair and rinsed out her mouth with some Listerine she found on a shelf, she really did feel better, with her queasiness gone and her mouth back to normal. And her stomach too. Even here in the bathhouse, she could smell something delicious cooking, and at the smell, she realized that she was ravenously hungry.

But as she headed out the swinging bathhouse door, someone on the other side was pushing in. Startled, Annie backed up as a dark, mustached young man came through, dressed only in baggy long underwear and a blue baseball cap. He wasn't very tall, but he was broad-shouldered and strong-looking with dark hair and bitter-chocolate brown eyes. The sight of Annie didn't seem to faze him.

"Howdy, there. I'm Robert Harry," he introduced himself and when he smiled, his whole face lit up with an almost electrical intensity, so that with perfect straight white teeth set off by his dark mustache, he was unexpectedly handsome. Because Annie had spent three years in the tinsel clutches of braces, teeth were the first thing she noticed about anyone.

"You must be the chief's daughter from the lower forty-eight," the young man said.

Annie was used to that expression, lower forty-eight meaning the forty-eight states south of Alaska. "Ah . . . yes . . . I'm Annie Sloane . . ." For some reason Annie couldn't seem to pull her act together. Maybe it was the bathhouse circumstances, or maybe it was because Robert was casually leaning against the sink in his scroungy-looking long underwear as if settling in for a chat. Annie realized now that he was about

Scott's age, nineteen or twenty, and not as old as she had first thought.

"Did Mac tell you that you're my rod man for the week? Just my luck. There's four of us in camp, and I had to draw the short straw so you and me are a team." Robert grinned at her. "And I'd say by the size of you, a short straw about sums it up."

Terrific. It was bad enough she had to go out in the field, but to top it off, she had to go out with this clown. And he seemed as enthusiastic about going out with her as she did with him. The bunch of them drew straws and the loser got her. Annie swelled with indignation. Just wait until she told Dad. But at the prospect, she immediately deflated. Dad would probably think it was funny, too.

Robert threw his towel over his shoulder and headed for the shower. "I don't want to be late for dinner. Willy Lou's a great cook, and we're having turkey tonight. After losing your lunch on the way out here, I betcha you're about ready for dinner too, Short Straw." With that, Robert flicked his towel against the sink and disappeared into a shower stall. Immediately, the cap was tossed out, the long johns were slung over the partition and the water was turned on.

Furious, Annie just stood glaring at the shower door. Behind those dark glasses and bored expression, Lester had seen her throw up and told everyone in camp. How could he? But she was even angrier at Robert. Short Straw, was she? She blew an irate blast of air out of her lungs, then abruptly turned on her heel and stalked out of the bathhouse, leaving Robert behind, sloshing in the shower and whistling an off-key tune.

5

Only one table was set up in the big tent that was the cook shack, with the other tables and chairs stacked on top of one another in a corner. Annie squeezed in beside her father at the end, and in spite of her earlier hunger, looked down at her plate in dismay. The woman behind the steam table had filled it with turkey, a mound of dressing, mashed potatoes, turnips, and peas, topping everything off with gravy.

"Hey there, everybody, you all know the chief, Frank Sloane, from the lower forty-eight, here to crack the whip over us, but you haven't met his daughter, Annie." Mac waved his fork around the table. "This-here is Robert Harry, your party chief. Lester you met in the helicopter and these other guys are Glenn Jones, Beers Mollani, Norman Tompkinson and Vladimir Peskov, better known as Val."

Lester and Robert she had certainly met, Lester with the big mouth, and Robert with the smart-aleck nicknames. At least Lester seemed to have gotten rid of his chewing tobacco. Either that, or he was eating around it. As for the rest of them, only one was clean-shaven. Otherwise, with their hairy faces and wool shirt sleeves rolled up to show long underwear un-

25

derneath, they looked like clones. They were probably nudging each other under the table right now and laughing at her from behind all that hair.

"And this is Willy Lou, the top buckaroo cook in the state." Mac indicated the tall, heavy, gray-haired woman who had dished out dinner and was now taking her place at the other end of the table.

Willy Lou, who wore a dirty white butcher apron over her blue jeans, had a Dutch bob haircut and crow's feet forking out from bright blue eyes that should have made her look jolly, like Mrs. Santa Claus, only somehow didn't. Random scars disfigured her face and the expression behind her thick glasses was noncommittal as she nodded in Annie's direction.

"Hi." Annie's greeting included everyone as she glanced around the table from under lowered eyes. They all looked so much alike she wondered how she would ever get their names straight, and in their rough, heavy clothes, they appeared so enormous, Annie felt smaller than ever.

"So how 'bout giving us a rundown on what's happening in the outside world, Frank? With the radio out, we haven't heard any news." Mac reached for the bowl of potatoes.

"What do you want, company news, Anchorage news, national news or just the baseball scores?"

"How about starting with the nuclear treaty with the Russians?" Mac poured gravy over his potatoes and dug in.

"Fortunately, it's still on," Dad began. "The President plans to meet in Geneva tomorrow with the Soviets for final talks after which they'll sign the treaty. It's hard to believe, but maybe we'll make it into the twenty-first century after all."

"Don't count on it. The Soviet Politburo is about as trustworthy as a grizzly coming out of his winter den." That was the one with the foreign name, Annie remembered, and his angry words were laced with an accent.

"I'm with Val. I don't trust a Commie bear any more'n I

trust a grizzly," one of the other men said, jabbing the air with his knife for emphasis. When Annie heard his deep voice, she realized he was older than the others and when she looked more closely, she saw gray sprinkled through his beard and hair. Glenn, she thought, that one was Glenn. "No sir, we're a little too close for comfort here, especially when you figure at the first sign of trouble, the Commies would blast our oil pipeline to kingdom come."

No, they won't, Annie protested silently. Not when the treaty is signed, they won't be blasting anything, not here, not the pipeline, not California.

The pale young man with the straggly blond beard laughed. He was so fair, his eyes seemed lashless and his eyebrows were only faint wisps. "Over to Eagle River Camp by the coast where I was working last summer, a bunch of us guys flew to Russia by chopper just to say we'd been there," he bragged, hooking his thumbs under his red suspenders and looking around the table with a self-satisfied expression.

Mac banged the table with his huge fist. "No, you don't, Beers. Not in my camp you don't try that kinda nonsense. I'd boot you outta here so fast you wouldn't know what hit you. Not that *Olyve Oil* would ever make it," he added.

"Don't be too sure, Mac," Robert spoke for the first time. "Lester took us for a joy ride the other night and we nearly made it to Hawaii. If we'd had more time, we'd have gone the whole way."

Annie was sure he was joking, but he looked so serious, she couldn't be certain. But immediately everyone started laughing and kidding around.

"Yeah, Hawaii."

"Man, those hula girls. Here we come."

"Sun, sand, surf and all them gorgeous bunnies." By process of elimination, that one had to be Norman. Norman had

27

a mop of curly brown hair that fell to his shoulders, and an equally full and curly brown beard.

And then dinner was over. Annie wouldn't have thought it was possible, but she had cleaned her plate.

"Hey, Willy Lou, what's for dessert?" Beers called out.

Willy Lou, who hadn't said a word all through dinner, stood up and wiped her hands on her apron. "Blueberry pie with ice cream," she snapped, as if daring anyone to complain.

But they did, all of them. "Ah, c'mon, Willy Lou, give us a break," Beers groaned and everyone joined in the grumbling.

"We're at the peak of our blueberry season so we're all pretty sick of 'em," Mac confided to Annie across the table as Willy Lou came back with the pie and another pot of coffee.

Unfortunately, over the coffee and pie, the conversation took a more personal turn. Mac asked what Elizabeth and Scott were doing these days and Dad was delighted to give him all the details. Scott would be a pre-med junior at Stanford next fall, coordinator of the Colleges for Nuclear Disarmament and captain of the soccer team. Elizabeth, who had graduated with honors from Stanford last spring after being a class officer for two years, would be starting graduate school in the fall. There was no doubt about it, Elizabeth and Scott were the answer to a parent's dream.

"What about you, Annie, what are you up to?" Mac asked.

Dad didn't give her a chance to answer. He put his arm around her shoulder and squeezed her affectionately. "Annie's doing fine. She's got another year of high school and then she'll be off to Stanford, too."

There was a moment of expectancy around the table as if everyone were waiting for Dad to continue. But that was it, there was nothing more to say, no achievements, no varsity letters, no class presidency, editorship of the yearbook, Honor Society, or even Cheer Squad.

28

Annie Annpins. All of a sudden, Annie remembered the nickname her grandmother had given her years ago. She felt the same way now, as small and insignificant as she had when she was five. But as she stared at her plate in embarrassment, she sensed someone's eyes on her, and when she glanced up, she saw Robert watching her, the angular lines of his face tempered by sympathy. Or was it pity? Annie felt herself blush as she looked away in confusion.

6

When Dad and Mac gave Annie an after-dinner tour, she realized that the camp wasn't a hodgepodge of tents and shacks after all, but a well-planned community with each tent serving a purpose and connected to every other tent by beaten paths. The biggest and most permanent tents were the cook shack and the office shack, both built on wooden platforms with aluminum arches covered by a nylon shell.

With only a skeleton crew, most of the twenty-three living tents were empty, but Annie had to admit that if the rest were like hers, they weren't bad. They were constructed on wooden frames with white canvas tops. Wooden doors, window flaps that opened and closed, mattresses set on raised platforms, rugs, tables, bookshelves, wall hangings and kerosene lamps made them at least comfortable, if not exactly a home away from home.

Mac pointed out the supply shed, the tool and electrical shed, the food storage shed, the helicopter maintenance shack near the landing pad and a shed set off by itself which he explained was filled with explosives for building the new landing strip. Since it had *Danger! Explosives!* painted all over it, Annie declined a closer inspection.

"Robert's our demolition expert," Mac explained. Robert, it seemed, was Little Salmon's jack of all trades.

Water was pumped into camp straight from the Lanatak River. "Here in the Brooks Range we drink the purest water in the world," Mac bragged. "Except that this blasted pump has been giving us trouble all summer," he added in an aside to Dad.

Dad laughed. "You've been managing camps long enough to know that if one thing doesn't conk out on you, something else will."

"Yeah, but the pump and the radio both?" Mac commented dryly, lighting a fresh cigar.

Electricity was supplied by a generator, but when Mac opened the door to the generator shed, Annie covered her ears and backed away. The roar and heat were like a blast from a furnace.

On to the core shed where Dad took over, opening the door with such a flourish Annie was anticipating something at least semi-interesting. But the shed was filled with nothing but long narrow boxes stacked one on top of another all the way to the ceiling. There must have been hundreds of them. Interesting or not, Annie could tell by her father's expression that she was in for it.

"The contents of these boxes represent the company's assets, Annie, worth millions, no more, maybe billions of dollars." He pulled out a box and opened it.

Annie peered inside and saw nothing but rows of two-foot-long gray cylindrical rock. "What do you mean, Dad?"

It was just the right question. "These drill core samples are what the exploration game is all about, Annie," her father explained. "First our geologists map the rocks and come up with areas of high lead and zinc potential. Next we do testing on a pattern laid out by our surveyors called grids. When we think we have something, we drill down and take out these rock core samples. The core is then cut in half, with half of it

31

sent off to be assayed, or analyzed, for mineral content, and the other half stored here in these boxes, all carefully logged as to mineral content and exact location."

Dad closed the box and replaced it on the shelf as if he were finished, but when Annie turned to go, he stopped her. "The analysis of the core tells us the percentage of lead and zinc in each sample so we know just where our richest ore concentration is," he continued. "If our competition ever got hold of these samples and their locations, they'd know as much about our mineral deposits as we do. That's one of the reasons we have a guard out here at camp all winter. 'Course the actual mining of the lead and zinc is a good ten years down the road, that is, if the deposits are worth mining at all."

Now Dad was finished. The core shed had obviously been the grande finale because as soon as they were outside, he and Mac said good night and headed for Mac's tent, talking business.

Annie, apparently, was on her own. Although the sun had swung all the way around to the northwest, it seemed reluctant to set, and the horizon was streaked with sweeping flames of pink and orange and red. Annie checked the time. Ten-thirty and still not dark. Idly, she wound her watch and looked around. Willy Lou was hanging out dish towels on a line behind the cook shack, Robert and Norman and Glenn were leaning against the office shack studying a map and arguing about something, Lester and Beers were washing down *Olyve Oil*. And that seemed to be the extent of the action.

As Annie started toward her own tent, a quick burst of flight down by the river caught her attention. Two ducks had swooped out of the sky, one brilliantly colored slate blue with a reddish body and white spots on its head. The other duck, dusky brown with the same white spots, must have been its mate. They called back and forth as they landed out of sight behind the willows that bordered the river.

32

They probably have a nest nearby, Annie thought, determined to get a closer look. She followed a path leading through the dense underbrush down to the water, quietly, oh so quietly, picking her way through the curving, snatching willow branches. A pump on the bank with a length of hose coming out of the river into one side of it and another length of hose leading from the pump up toward camp was humming away, and even Annie, unmechanical as she was, realized that this must be the water pump.

The ducks were resting on a rock in the middle of the river preening themselves like a fussy middle-aged couple preparing for bed. Annie settled down to watch. From here she couldn't see the camp or even hear the constant background drone of the generator. All she could hear was the faint on-again-off-again purr of the water pump and the rush of the sparkling river that was so clear she could see the shape and color of every rock on its bottom. A huge hawk circled gracefully overhead as the two ducks dropped into the water and drifted with the current. The sun, throwing out its last rays in an attempt to hold back the night, lit up the sky with a fireworks display of brilliant shifting patterns. The mountains in the distance looked black in the shaded half-light, ancient and changeless. The immense silence and the drama of the sky were wild, enormous, overwhelming, and Annie felt her breath quicken as she suddenly experienced the power of this unique country. She picked up a rounded rock from the riverbank and rubbed her hand over its smoothness.

"Grr."

Annie froze. The deep-gut sound was low, hard to differentiate from the rush of the river. Gripping the rock tight in her hand, she strained to listen, but the moving water and the nearby pump were the only sounds she heard.

"Grrr."

This time there was no mistaking the throaty snarl. It was

33

definitely an animal and it was closer, coming from somewhere in back of her. Without realizing it, Annie focused on the two ducks still bobbing downstream like colorful decoys. She was watching the ducks, but in her mind's eye, all she could see was a silvery hulk with a distinguishing hump, poised in the brush behind her. Annie's heart took a run of thumping beats, then stopped altogether.

"Grrr."

Again. But this time it sounded different, almost human, with a snort at the end of it like smothered laughter. Annie spun around, still terrified, but no longer totally paralyzed. And there he was. Robert. Down on all fours peering out of the willows.

"Grrr." He tried to growl again, but he was laughing too hard.

Annie choked and sputtered incoherently, her face crimson. "You . . . you . . . how could you . . ." Now that the danger was past, her heart was racing so fast, it almost leapt out of her chest.

"Oh, Short Straw, I couldn't help it. You wouldn't deny me that once-in-a-lifetime opportunity, would you?"

Annie didn't answer. She just brushed past Robert and headed up the path at what she hoped was a dignified pace, trailed the whole way by the sound of his rocking laughter. She'd go straight to bed, that's what. It was the only place she could get away from Robert, and the best way she knew to get this whole awful day over with.

7

Annie was awake on and off all night, aware of when Willy Lou climbed in her sleeping bag on the other side of the tent, aware of the stifling heat blasting out of the heater, aware of the sounds of camp, the constant generator drone, the splash of the distant river, low male voices and the rustling and scratching of small animals beyond the tent.

Although it was never completely dark except for an hour or two during the heart of the night, at some point past three o'clock, dawn began to lighten the northeast sky. The birds had already started up their early morning chorus when Annie heard a wonderful sound, the tip-tap of rain on the canvas roof. At first it was just a gentle drizzle, but as the minutes passed, the tempo increased until it was a steady downpour. There would be no going out in the field today. Annie's tension eased in an almost physical release and she fell fast asleep.

It was Willy Lou's alarm that woke her, persistent, shrill, annoying. A groan escaped from the mound that was Willy Lou as a hand reached out and clicked it off. Willy Lou pulled herself up to a sitting position, put on her eyeglasses, and looked over at Annie with a scowl.

"Mornin'," she mumbled. A wide yawn creased the scars on her face into deep ridges so that her face produced the same effect as the tundra patterned by its braided streams and creeks. "You'd better get crackin'. Robert likes to be in the field early 'n Lester flies his first crew out at seven."

Annie could still hear the rain tapping on the canvas overhead and there was a wet spot on the floor where water had leaked through. "But it's raining," she said.

"So I noticed." Unsympathetic.

"We won't work in the rain, will we?"

Willy Lou had already put on her blue jeans and a wool shirt over long white underwear that made her appear larger than ever from Annie's sleeping-bag vantage point. "Be thankful it ain't snow. We got three inches last Friday," was Willy Lou's non-answer answer.

As soon as Willy Lou had left, Annie got up and numbly dressed. Yanking her thick curly hair into a ponytail with an elastic band, she waited until the coast was clear, then made a run for the outhouse and bathhouse through the puddles that had already accumulated on the paths. It was raining all right, a steady, gray, cold rain lashed by gusty winds.

Her father was waiting for her by the cook shack. "Your big day, huh, Annie? Too bad it's raining but the sky's clear to the west, so here's hoping."

Annie didn't respond. There was nothing to say. Dad wouldn't let a little rain stop him and it didn't occur to him that a little rain would stop her. There was some grumbling and complaining about the weather in the chow line, but it was all pretty good-natured. With her mind on the day ahead, Annie didn't join in the kidding, nor did she even notice how much food Willy Lou had stacked on her tray, a bowl of hot cereal, scrambled eggs, sausage, homemade rolls, juice and coffee. Dad led the way to a table where the men were already digging in as if they'd never seen food before.

"Howdy." Dad spoke to each man in turn, adding a slap on the back as he passed Mac.

Everyone acknowledged the greeting with a pleasant, "Hey, there, Frank," or "Howdy," with a smile and a nod to Annie, all except Robert, who winked as she sat down across from him. What she didn't need right now was a wink, especially from Robert. That was some shabby trick he'd pulled on her last night, and what little sleep she had gotten had been filled with growling nightmares.

"We didn't used to eat like this in my day," Dad said as he started in on his eggs.

"Willy Lou's the best camp cook in the state," Mac boasted. "We got roast beef and Yorkshire pudding for dinner tonight."

"Too bad I'll have to miss it," Dad commented without missing a bite.

Startled, Annie looked up. "What do you mean? Where will you be?"

Dad returned Annie's look, his eyes the same gray-green as hers. "I'm really sorry, Annie, but there's a legal problem that's come up that I have to handle in Anchorage and I'll fly the radio back to Kotz for repairs at the same time. Mac and I discussed every alternative so that I could stay here with you, but I'm the only one who can take care of the Anchorage business. I won't be gone long, only until the end of the week."

Until the end of the week! Annie gasped out loud, and then, embarrassed, glanced around to see if anyone had noticed. But no one even seemed interested except Robert, who was grinning at her from under the brim of his blue cap. "I could come to Anchorage with you," she quickly offered.

"Annie, I wouldn't deprive you of this experience for anything in the world, certainly not for some boring business meetings. No, everything's set here and Mac is counting on you, right, Mac?"

"Right." Mac smiled, his gold front tooth startling in the middle of so much red beard.

Annie gripped the edge of the table. "But . . . but . . . that's okay . . . I wouldn't mind . . . I can get ahead on my summer reading . . ." It sounded stuttery and feeble but it was the best she could do. Stunned as she was, she knew she couldn't burst out with the truth, that she was afraid, that she didn't want the experience, and didn't want to be counted on either.

"Actually there isn't room for you in the plane, Annie. I have to take some equipment back that Little Salmon is finished with, plus all the garbage." Dad sounded matter of fact, just as if Annie's world weren't falling apart.

"Yeah, we got enough garbage to start a landfill mountain," Glenn said, talking around a pipe he was trying to light.

Baffled, Annie looked from Dad to Glenn back to Dad again. This garbage nonsense must be some kind of in-joke she didn't understand.

Mac noticed her expression. "We can't bury our garbage because of government regulations so we store it in plastic bags and fly it out. Garbage lying around is a big attraction for animals, especially bears."

Annie could hardly believe her ears. There wasn't room for her in the plane because it was filled with garbage. What Mom had said was true, that as soon as Dad hit Alaska, he reverted to his old mountain man personality. Look at him now. His wool shirt sleeves were rolled up to show his long underwear, and he had already started growing a stubble of a beard.

Tears of frustration filled Annie's eyes and she knew if she didn't leave they would spill over in an embarrassing flood. She picked up her practically untouched breakfast tray and headed for the kitchen. She didn't notice Robert following her until he whispered in her ear.

"With that bushy ponytail of yours, from the back you look like a little red fox bobbing along. 'Course most of the foxes around here have rabies." He laughed. "Not that you don't look a little rabid yourself right now."

Annie didn't even turn around. It was bad enough that Dad was leaving and that she had to fly out in the field in the rain, but what topped it all off was that she had to go out with this joker.

8

Dad walked Annie to the helicopter to see her off. "You've got everything you need in your backpack, Annie?"

She nodded. She ought to. Dad had packed it for her, matches, a knife, compass, toilet paper, a space blanket, a wool shirt and lunch.

"Keep yourself open to the experience and I promise you'll remember this week the rest of your life," Dad said. "And Mac tells me that Robert is trustworthy, his most reliable man, with good common sense," he added, as if he suddenly needed reassurance, too.

A hard hug and a goodbye kiss and Annie was inside the cocoon of noise that was *Olyve Oil*, seated behind Lester and Robert. The blades changed pitch and the thump-thump-thump of their vibration pulsed like a monstrous metronome. The rain splashed down the curved panes as Annie looked out the window. Her father was standing about fifty feet away, his face hidden in the shadows of his rain hood. Then, as *Olyve Oil* lifted off in a blast of wind, he held onto his hood with one hand and gave a thumbs-up salute with his other. A moment later, he was out of sight.

The sound of the engine and the blades consumed the whole space with no pockets left over for talking. That suited Annie fine. She had nothing to say, certainly not to Robert, so she spent the time staring out the window as the tundra unfolded beneath them, flat, treeless, still green, but already patched with the russets and reds of fall, and sculpted with braided streams and brooding blue-black ponds.

Robert turned around in his seat, tapped her knee and pointed down. "Caribou," he shouted.

Automatically, Annie looked down. Alarmed by the roar of the helicopter, fifteen or twenty caribou bounded across the tundra, their wide antlers ungainly and their rumps and tails flags of white.

"Barren ground caribou," Robert yelled. "Last summer a hundred thousand of 'em took three days to pass camp in migration. They were in bunches and clumps, but the herd was thirty miles long and seven miles wide. Ain't that so, Lester?"

"Yup, we measured 'em from the air." The wad of chewing tobacco was back in Lester's mouth so that his beard seemed to be moving of its own volition.

Annie wasn't certain which bothered her more, Lester's tobacco, or Robert's "ain't." When they had talked in the bathhouse, Robert's grammar had been fine. It was as if he did it to be one of the boys, the way Dad was growing a beard and mustache. At least he was being civil to her. Maybe he was trying to make up for last night, as well as for that crack this morning at breakfast.

Whoop, all of a sudden, the helicopter took a steep lift upward, just clearing a mountaintop before it dipped down on the other side, leaving Annie's stomach somewhere back on the tundra with the caribou. She immediately closed her eyes and leaned her head back. She couldn't be sick today, she just couldn't. Not only did she not see any barf bags, but she was

41

also determined not to be sick in front of either Robert or Lester, especially Robert.

Annie flew that way, with her head back and her eyes closed, for a long time, just fighting to keep her stomach under control. And then she realized they were dropping vertically for a landing. But it was much too soon. She certainly didn't want to stay in the helicopter, but she didn't want to get out of it either. Not that she had a choice. They were down in that surprisingly easy way Lester had of landing. Robert flipped his rain hood up over his baseball cap, shouldered his backpack and climbed out.

Panicked, Annie unbuckled her seat belt, grabbed her own pack and scrambled out too, running in a crouch like Robert away from the helicopter. Behind her, *Olyve Oil* took off with a roar that blasted her rain hood right off. But Lester had left without any discussion of where he would pick them up. Although they were close to a gray limestone mountain, it looked like every other gray limestone mountain. They weren't far from a little stream bordered by scrubby willows, but it was identical to every other little stream bordered by scrubby willows.

"C'mon." Robert, who obviously wasn't concerned, waved her on. Annie gave one last reluctant look back at *Olyve Oil* as it ricocheted off the ceiling of low gray clouds like a bouncing ball, then rushed to catch up.

Not only was it raining, but it was cold too, and a wind swept across the treeless flats with nothing to break it. Annie snapped on her rain hood as cold drops splatted against her. Her gloves were in her backpack and as soon as they stopped, she'd get them out, but not now. Annoyed as she was at Robert, right now she didn't want to be more than a foot away from him. Whether he liked it or not, they were bonded for the day.

Only it didn't quite work out that way. When Mac had said

42

that Annie was running rod for Robert, she hadn't even considered what that might mean. Now she found out. With his survey equipment, Robert posted himself at the control station on top of a talus slope that erupted out of the tundra like a gray wart. Annie was left down on the ground with her hands full. In one hand she carried twenty three-foot-long wooden stakes tied with orange ribbons. In her other hand, she held a prism, a set of mirrors that looked like three beer cans arranged in a triangle and attached to a pole. Robert hooked a hand radio like his on her belt, showed her how to use it, and then from the control station, radioed down directions as to where she should place the stakes that he called laths. As soon as she was in position, he aimed his laser survey gun at her prism, and when her mirrors reflected back his laser beam, he was able to make accurate measurements as to the map distance, the real distance and the vertical distance.

What it meant was that Annie was out in the field alone, with Robert at the control station on top of the mountain giving her orders where to go. At first she tried to keep an eye out for anything large and silvery, especially behind her, but the terrain was so difficult to walk on, particularly wearing the high rubber boots that Dad called Alaskan sneakers, she finally had to concentrate completely on that. From the air, the tundra had looked flat, but close up, it was soggy and wet, with tussocks of sedge that didn't support any weight. The first time Annie stepped on one, it gave way under her and she slipped off it, twisting her ankle in the muck, and right away she realized how easy it would be to break an ankle or even a leg out here. At least the rain had eased up so she could take off her rain hood and widen her vision.

"Go due north three hundred feet," Robert ordered over the radio.

Which way was north? Annie circled helplessly a moment. Although Robert had showed her how to use her compass, her hands were too full to dig it out, and without it, she had no concept of where north was.

"Turn left," came Robert's exasperated voice.

Annie started walking, taking short steps and counting to three hundred the way Robert had told her. Her throat was dry and sore from swallowing so much and her legs felt rubbery, not only from the effort of walking on what seemed to be a field of slippery soccer balls, but also from the tension she was working under. Even though Robert had assured her he had a perfect view of the countryside and everything in it, what good was all his common sense up there on top of a mountain?

Swish. A rattling cry and a clapping of wings right in front of Annie startled her so she cried out. A little brown-and-white bird like a chicken flew up almost in her face before taking off with a loud drumming of its wings. It didn't seem possible that anything so small could produce such a racket. Annie had to stop and wait until her breathing started up in a normal way again.

There was a chuckle from the radio. "That was a ptarmigan. They always scare me when I flush them out, too."

When Annie looked back up at Robert, he was waving at her and somehow she felt better.

But by noon, every muscle in her body ached and her legs were trembling. She was so tense from looking down at her feet to see where she was going, as well as constantly looking behind her, she was as exhausted as she had ever been in her life. It wasn't that she didn't see plenty of wildlife, because she did, and plenty of dead life, too, bones of every size and shape, and bleached, white antlers that caribou had shed over the years. Although the live caribou, grazing peacefully in groups of threes or fours, luckily seemed to keep their distance, mice and voles and even a good-sized hare scurried across her path as she moved from one place to another.

It seemed strange that with no trees there were so many

birds, but Annie spotted robins and sparrows and ravens and hawks which she recognized, and all sorts of other birds which she didn't. She saw lots of tiny wildflowers too, miniature yellow poppies and creeping dogwood and crimson-centered silver stars, as well as great stretches of grass topped with fluffy white puffs that looked like cotton.

And because Robert had been giving her precise directions the whole time, she had to keep her mind on that too. It was a long morning of barely controlled panic, and when Robert radioed her to return to the mountain for lunch, she hardly had the strength to make it.

He was waiting for her with that teasing grin on his face, looking as rested as when they had started. But why shouldn't he be rested? He had been standing around all morning in one spot while she'd done all the work and taken all the risks. She must have walked a hundred miles out in that boggy tundra and how she had managed to avoid a broken ankle, she couldn't imagine.

Robert put his arm around her shoulders and gave her a hug. "You'll feel better when you get a little chow in your belly, Short Straw," he said, "and this afternoon I promise we'll have better weather. Take a look at that."

Annie glanced up. Although it was still raining a fine mist, the gray cloud cover had parted and with the sun peeking around its edges, a spectacular, glorious double rainbow arched from one mountain peak to another.

9

The double rainbow was a good sign. The rain stopped, the wind died down and the sun even came out and began to dry everything up, including Annie. And food really did make her feel better. Willy Lou had packed turkey sandwiches, a container of potato salad, a bag of Fritos, an apple and cookies in her lunch sack and Annie ate it all. Since she was trying to gain weight, she usually had to force herself to eat, but not today.

She and Robert spread their space blankets out of the wind on the sunny side of the mountain. The space blankets, about seven feet by five feet, were red waterproof tarp on one side and reflective aluminum on the other that folded up into tiny squares that fit neatly into their packs.

Annie would just as soon have been quiet and rested, but right away, Robert started talking. "Those mountains to the north of us are part of the Brooks Range. It's one of the few mountain ranges in the world that runs east and west instead of north and south."

Since they seemed to be the only two people left on the face of the earth, Annie suddenly couldn't see much point in staying angry at Robert. She turned around and there, in the distance, was the mostly unexplored wilderness of snowy peaks and valleys that was the Brooks Range.

"Over there, to the west is the Chukchi Sea that separates Alaska from Russia," Robert said as he opened his bag of Fritos and ate a handful. "Alaskans feel different about Russia than the rest of the country. It's just a little too close for comfort, and everyone over 50 remembers when the Japanese invaded Alaska during World War II and held a couple of the Aleutian Islands for a year. Yup, Alaska's a whole lot more exposed than the lower forty-eight."

Annie looked at the cold and forbidding strip of water in the distance and shivered. She hadn't realized before just how close Russia was. "Then there's nothing between us and Russia but water and tundra."

Robert laughed as he crumpled up his Frito bag and started in on his apple. "What do you mean, nothing but tundra? Just because there ain't trees don't mean it's nothing. There's more life in an acre of tundra than ten square miles of anyplace else."

As if to verify Robert's statement, a little ground squirrel scooted across the path in front of them. It looked like a large yellowish-gray chipmunk and was just as appealing. It ran down the slope almost to the bottom, then suddenly stood up on its hind legs and gave a chirpy squeal. Annie had heard that same little squeal on and off all morning and hadn't been able to figure out where it was coming from. Now she realized it was these little squirrels and she couldn't help laughing.

"We call them sik-siks because that's what their whistle sounds like."

"Sik-sik. Yeah, it does," Annie agreed.

Annie's laughter encouraged Robert. "I like to think I'm the first person who ever walked this land, the last real wilderness

47

on earth, untouched since time began. Solitude, that's what it's all about."

Robert was almost likeable when he talked like that, one human being to another instead of straining to act macho, with his teasing and his "ain'ts" and bad grammar. And his eyes were about the most expressive eyes Annie had ever seen, one moment dark and hidden and the next, like now, open and laughing with golden lights.

Suddenly Annie was aware that Robert was returning her look with those incredible eyes boring into hers and she self-consciously finished eating her cookies.

"Well, someone must have been around where I was working this morning," she said. "There are paths like motorcycle trails all over the place."

At Robert's smile, she immediately felt as defensive as a child. "Tundra looks tough, but it's fragile," he explained. "Anything that breaks down the thin ground cover of the tundra like caribou or a bulldozer will leave scars that last for years. What you saw are trails the migrating caribou made, probably years ago. Other animals use 'em too, bears, wolves, wolverines, marmots, me. See, here on these talus slopes, they make a nice ledge like a ramp to walk on. I follow any caribou highways I can find."

Mentioning all those wild animals without even a change of expression! "I don't see how you can stand the danger of working up here," Annie blurted out as she stared over the vast desolation, the rolling tundra intersected with ponds and streams and rimmed by dark, white-maned mountains.

"What's the danger? See, I carry a .44 magnum. It's not as effective as a sawed-off shotgun, but it'll do at close range." Robert pulled back his jacket, and there, tucked in a shoulder holster, was a big gun. It was the verification of all of Annie's fears and she stared at it.

"Besides," Robert went on, "you got more chance of getting

killed in a New York subway than around here. Missoula, Montana, is about as much city as I ever want to see."

Annie was distracted in spite of herself. "Is that where you're from?"

"Nah, I'm from Kotzebue, right here in Alaska, but I'm getting my B.S. in geology from the University of Montana in Missoula. Then I'll work up here permanent." Robert heaved his apple core as far as he could, then looked over at Annie sitting beside him, her arms clasping her knees tight to her chest. He studied her a moment as if he were making up his mind. "Did you know that I'm part Inupiat?"

Annie turned and looked into Robert's eyes, serious now. "What do you mean?"

Robert grinned but his expression stayed sober. "Native Alaskan, Eskimo, whatever you want to call it. Both my father and mother are part Inupiat."

Although there was no reason for Annie to be surprised, she was. She swallowed, trying to think of something appropriate to say, but nothing came to her and there was silence between them as she watched a distant hawk cruise overhead, catching the thermals and effortlessly gliding higher and higher.

"Some of my people say I'm selling out because I'm going to be a geologist and explore and develop land they think should never be developed. My father especially is angry at me." Robert sounded unsure of himself as he picked up a rock and tossed it from one hand to the other. All Annie could see was his lowered profile and she realized with a start that he had a crooked bump in his nose where it must have once been broken.

"Still, Short, I had to make my own decision. The old ways may have been good once, but there's no stopping what's happening to Alaska. Exploration and development are here and anyone who thinks different is kidding himself." Robert's voice was stronger as if this were a point he had argued before.

"Your father's company cares about us natives and our land and that's why I signed up with them. Since it's going to be developed, it might as well be done the best way possible. So that's it. Sometimes you have to buck what everyone else thinks you should do, just to survive on your own as a person."

It was a long speech and when Robert was finished, he smoothed out his mustache in an embarrassed sort of gesture and tilted his head at Annie as if challenging her to contradict him.

Annie had no intention of contradicting. Maybe bucking what everyone wanted was okay for Robert, but it wasn't for her. Her family was all she had, and nothing was worth risking a break with them.

Robert reached over and squeezed her knee. "Don't look so gloomy, Short. I haven't sold my soul and no one's asking you to renounce your throne or kiss a frog. Now come on, I want to work on the other side of the mountain this afternoon, so let's clean up our lunch trash and get going. You've heard the saying, if a pine needle falls in the forest, a deer will hear it, an eagle will see it and a bear will smell it, and we don't need any bears smelling what's left of our turkey sandwiches."

We certainly don't, Annie silently agreed as she picked up every crumb and paper she could find and stuffed them in her backpack.

Somehow Annie got through the afternoon, though by the time Robert radioed her that they were going to call it a day, she was stiff from her neck all the way down her back from the hours-long effort of twisting and turning to keep alert in every direction at once, as well as maneuvering around the maddening tussocks. It didn't seem possible that anyone could stand up to this country, defy it, pace it off, survey it. It was all she could do to keep from being swallowed up and devoured by it.

Robert had spread out Annie's space blanket at the bottom of the same talus slope where they had eaten lunch. "Long day, huh?" he commiserated.

Annie nodded as she gingerly eased herself down onto the blanket. Although it was only four o'clock, she felt as if she'd been working eighty hours instead of eight.

"Lester won't be showing up until five, but I thought you'd like to break early on your first day." Robert's smile held no hint of teasing.

"How will Lester find us?" She had forgotten all about that basic problem.

"As soon as you see the helicopter, you picture it as a horizontal clock with the nose at twelve o'clock. If Lester flies in perpendicular, you radio him that you're at three o'clock or nine o'clock, or whatever. If he's coming right at you, you radio him that you're at twelve o'clock. Then you give the approximate mileage and add, I'm up on the hill or down in the creek, or wherever. It's never failed yet," Robert explained in his old matter-of-fact, cool-guy voice with all the earlier vulnerability gone. That was okay. Annie had heard it and knew it was there, regardless.

"How come we switched to the other side of the mountain this afternoon without finishing up what we started this morning?" Annie, who didn't really care, yawned so deeply her jaw cracked.

"While we were eating lunch I noticed a bear cache."

At the tone of Robert's voice, Annie sat up straighter. "What's that?"

"When a grizzly kills a sik-sik or a marmot or something small, he eats it on the spot. But he prefers his meat a little rotten so when he's lucky enough to get himself a caribou or moose, he buries what he doesn't eat and comes back to it later. And it ain't smart to get between a bear and his cache. Didn't you notice that big mound of dirt and twigs and brush a coupl'a hundred yards out?"

Annie shook her head numbly. She'd been working all morning around a bear cache and didn't even know it.

"Steaming bear scat's something else to watch out for."

Robert casually pulled his unopened package of cookies from his pack and started to eat them.

"What's b . . . bear scat?"

"You know, bear droppings, dump, crap, whatever you want to call it. This time of year when the bears are filling up on blueberries, it looks something like a blueberry pie. And if you see one steaming, that means it's fresh and you'd better watch out."

"But . . . but I didn't notice . . . I didn't know . . ."

Robert raised his arms over his square shoulders in his own stretching yawn. "It's no big deal. Nothin' happened, so forget it." Robert straightened out his space blanket, then lay down on it, wrapping the aluminum side tight around him.

Annie watched, incredulous. "What are you doing?"

"I'm gonna take a nap before Lester comes. The aluminum side reflects body heat and warms everything up real good." With that, Robert closed his eyes and as far as Annie could tell, fell fast asleep.

It was hard to believe. Only two people left in the world surrounded by bear caches and bear scat and one of them was asleep. Annie shuddered, cold right through her layers of clothing to the marrow of her bones. She'd have to sit guard, that's all, and if anything showed up, she'd wake Robert and let him handle it . . . Robert and his gun. Even now she could see the bulge of it through his jacket as he breathed in and out peacefully. He even snored the same breathy little wheeze as Willy Lou's.

Annie was shivering hard now. They had been sitting on the protected side of the mountain, but the wind had shifted and was blowing right toward them. Tentatively she lay down on her own space blanket and folded it around her the way Robert had. Not that she was going to sleep. Far from it. It was just that she needed to warm up. Nevertheless, within minutes, Annie, too, was asleep, her deep breathing in almost perfect rhythm with Robert's.

10

The next two days in the field went along pretty much like the first, except that now Annie knew enough to keep an eye out for bear caches, which she didn't see again, as well as bear scat, which she didn't see either, cold or steaming. What with her adrenaline pumping like crazy all day, as well as trying to act halfway intelligent in response to Robert's directions from the control station, it was the longest two days she could ever remember. Almost as soon as Lester picked them up at night and she was inside *Olyve Oil*, she fell asleep. Still, despite her exhaustion, Annie began to feel good about herself, about getting up before six, working hard all day, doing a respectable job, and, not the least of it, earning good pay.

But on the fourth morning, Annie woke to a silence that was so thick, it almost obliterated the sound of the generator. Willy Lou was already out of bed, pulling on a parka over her sweater. She looked at Annie with a wry expression on her broad face.

"Snow. Could be worse. Could be sleet," she announced as she opened the door and disappeared into the whiteness.

Snow. In the middle of August. Annie closed her eyes. She

ached all over, her legs, her back, her shoulders. Even her head ached. Just the thought of going out in the snow tired her. Still, snow or no snow, she had better be on time today or Robert would be at her like he was yesterday when Lester had taken the other survey team out into the field first because she had been late. At breakfast she had gotten caught up in listening to an argument between Mac and Val about the nuclear disarmament treaty and had forgotten the time.

Annie groaned and eased herself out of her sleeping bag. As she mechanically pulled her blue jeans on over the long underwear she hadn't changed since she had arrived, she rehashed the discussion. Val had pounded his fist on the table. The Soviet government is incapable of keeping its word. The treaty won't be worth the paper it's printed on, he had insisted. Mac had disagreed. We have to give it a chance, and after all, the Commies have stuck to the year's moratorium on nuclear stockpiling.

Val has to be wrong, Annie told herself as she brushed her hair back and pulled it into the snarly ponytail she'd adopted. The treaty is the only chance we have if we don't want the world blown to bits, she reasoned as she stretched to work out the stiffness. Maybe coffee would wake her up. Before she came up here, she didn't even like coffee. Now here she was, like everyone else in camp, filling her coffee cup before she even thought of food.

When Annie stepped outside, she saw that the sun was already a yellowish globe in a jaundiced sky and the snow was coming down in lazy flakes almost as big as Christmas tree ornaments. All in all, the storm didn't seem very serious.

Then, as she started toward the cook shack, she noticed the whole crew, including Willy Lou already swathed in her huge apron, lined up beyond the tool shed, intently watching something across the river. Just by their rapt concentration, Annie had a sudden rush of insight that she wasn't sure that she wanted to know what they were looking at. Nevertheless, she was drawn toward the silent group, cautious step by cautious step. No one noticed her except Norman, who nudged her with his elbow and pointed across the river.

Annie peered past Norman's long wild hair. At first she didn't see anything, just the clear blue Lanatak River bounded on either bank by thick willows. But a quick movement on the other side of the water, a flash of gray and brown, focused her attention and her jaw went slack with shock.

A grizzly bear, silhouetted against the snow on the side of a low talus slope, was playing with something, batting it up in the air with its paw the way Scott used to play with an old baseball with the stuffing coming out. Only this was an animal, not a baseball, a silvery brown marmot the size of a small dog. Annie had seen a marmot colony just yesterday, humps and bumps and tunnels ridging through the side of a mountain, with a marmot sentinel sitting up on its hind legs standing guard. When the marmot had seen Annie, it had shrieked its alarm with an almost human whistle before darting into one of the burrow entrances. With its little black-and-white masked face and its wonderful whistle, Annie had found it enchanting, and so was Robert's name for it, a whistle pig.

Although this marmot was dead and no doubt about it, the bear, which could smash open the skull of a moose with one blow, was tossing it up and cuffing it with incredible dexterity. The bear never looked over at its mesmerized audience or acknowledged in any way that it knew they were there, but its message came across loud and clear. All this, you, your camp, your tents, your helicopter, have no place here, don't belong here and never will.

Now the bear flipped the marmot over and got down to the serious business of eating. As soon as it had devoured the marmot, it turned its back on its audience and casually stuffed almost an entire blueberry bush in its mouth before ambling

55

away. A light dusting of snow whitened its silvery brown coat and the weight it had gained for the coming winter rounded its body with layers of fat.

Annie didn't remember running back to her tent, but all of a sudden, there she was, cold and trembling. She pulled off her boots, scrambled up onto her bunk, slid into her sleeping bag, and squeezed her eyes shut to block out what she had just seen. The door squeaked open and Annie heard a heavy tread across the flimsy wooden floorboards, but she didn't open her eyes, not even when someone sat down on the edge of her bunk.

"When me and my husband Marvin moved to Alaska after World War II, I thought it was the most godforsaken country I'd ever seen, and when a husky dog did this to my face, I almost left both Marvin and Alaska. But I stuck it out and though I've been a widow a long time now, I can't imagine living anywhere else. Alaska's a country that opens the soul."

Annie was so startled to hear all those words coming out of Willy Lou that she opened her eyes just to make sure that it was Willy Lou. It was indeed. Willy Lou's face looked as impassive as ever as she took off her glasses and cleaned them with a dirty-looking rag. Without her glasses, her scarred face again reminded Annie of the tundra with its pitted game trails and braided streams, although now that she knew how it had happened, she felt a wrench of sympathy.

"That old bear out there's no threat to anyone," Willy Lou went on. "He was perfectly happy with his plaything and he ain't about to bother me or you, and 'course we were upwind to him." Willy Lou's mouth turned up just a fraction at the edges in what was almost a smile.

Annie shook her head and was surprised that her eyes were wet. Those hateful tears! "It's not just the bear, it's everything. Dad made me come up here to toughen me up, but it won't work. I hate it . . . I'm afraid . . ." The words spilled out in a breathless tumble.

56

Now Willy Lou was smiling, but not in a mocking way. Her expression looked almost soft. "Your pa wants you to be an eagle and you're just a little snow bunting. Your pa oughtta know that eagles are only scavengers and bad-tempered bullies that don't do much but look impressive, while snow buntings aren't very impressive looking at all, but they're one of the few songbirds we got in Alaska, a friendly little bird with a joyful call like a flute that adds to the world just by being. Now you wash up your face and I'll get you a cup'a coffee for the ride out in *Olyve Oil*. You know how itchy Robert gets if he's second team out."

Annie clutched her hands together for courage and shook her head so imperceptibly it was hardly noticeable. "I'm not going out today . . ." She lowered her eyelids so she wouldn't have to look into Willy Lou's penetrating blue eyes, afraid that the force of them might compel her to change her mind. But Willy Lou didn't say anything. She just sat there a moment, then stood up, pulled the sleeping bag closer around Annie's shoulders and tiptoed out, leaving Annie in a state of suspended surprise that she had really said no, as well as amazement that Willy Lou had seemed to understand. And care.

11

Robert wasn't quite so understanding. He stood at the foot of Annie's bunk and scowled at her with his thundery dark eyebrows. His jacket hung open so that the gun in its holster shone metallic and threatening.

"Listen to me, Short Straw. I'm on full scholarship at Montana and I need this job bad. The company considers me a native which means I gotta be twice as good as anyone else to get half the credit. And right now I need you running rod for me."

Annie didn't allow herself to look at Robert or fully hear what he was saying. All she knew was that she wouldn't, couldn't, go out in the field.

"You're it or nothing, Short."

It was as if she were a puppet and Robert was pulling the strings. Annie felt her eyes being drawn to his face and by the familiar hard knot in her stomach, she knew she would end up doing what he wanted, getting out of bed, boarding *Olyve Oil*, and flying out into the field. But before she could say anything, there was a knock, the door opened and Mac stepped in. He was smiling. At least under his mass of red beard, it looked like a smile.

"I'm glad you're both here. I got a surprise for you, a day off." Mac's usually mellow voice was loud and unnaturally hearty. "Robert can finish up some paperwork this morning, then this afternoon, the two of you can mud tub down the river."

Robert frowned. "Did Willy Lou put you up to this?"

Mac shrugged. "She figured since Annie was only going to be here another coupl'a days, she might as well enjoy it. And I agree with her."

Robert didn't answer. He just glared at Annie, then at Mac, then back at Annie. Without a word, he turned on his heel and left the tent, slamming the door behind him.

Mac's grin was wide enough to reveal his gold front tooth. "He'll come around once he simmers down."

Annie had no idea what they were talking about. "What's a mud tub?"

Mac already had his hand on the doorknob. "It's a big galvanized steel tub like a bathtub that we use as holding tanks for drilling lubricants. Two people fit in a tub real nice and Glenn even built paddles and two seats in the tub to make it more comfortable. You and Robert can paddle downstream seven or eight miles, then Lester can fly down later in *Olyve Oil* and pick up both you and the tub."

Paddling down the river in a tub certainly sounded safer than working out in the field. "Okay," Annie agreed.

So Annie spent the morning in her tent. She read for a while, then climbed back in her sleeping bag and slept. Maybe it was the dry heat blasting out of the Preway heater that knocked her out so completely, but when she got up for lunch, she still felt groggy. And embarrassed to face Robert.

But Robert was surprisingly pleasant. He came right over with his lunch tray and sat down next to her. "I hate to admit it, Short, but I really did need to catch up on my paperwork. Now that it's done I can take you fishing. The char are running and Willy Lou says if we catch enough, she'll cook them for dinner. Char are a great game fish, a combination of a trout and a salmon."

"What about the mud tub?"

"We can do that later. Lester flew the tub down from the drill rig this morning. After dinner we can paddle down the Lanatak a couple of miles, if you want to."

So fishing it was. Robert brought her fishing tackle, a rod, lures, creel, everything she would possibly need. But for the first couple of hours, Annie just sat on the sun-warmed gravel bank of the Lanatak River and watched Robert. The snow had melted, all except on the far mountains, and the water sparkled clear rushing blue so that its rocky bottom seemed to ripple just below the surface. Gradually Annie relaxed and gave herself over to the sunny afternoon. Robert, stripped down to his jeans, a shirt and a pair of red suspenders, stood nearby intently casting into the water over and over. He seemed so serious, and so oblivious to her, Annie impulsively scrambled up the bank and ducked behind some willows.

"Grrr," she snarled. "Grrr."

Robert spun around, his eyes wide. Although it only took him a moment to register, in that moment a flash of surprise crossed his face. And then, as Annie came crawling out of the brush, still growling, he started to laugh.

"Grrr . . . grrr . . ."

"You're right, Short, I deserved that," he had to admit as Annie, laughing too, stood up and brushed herself off.

"Hey, Robert, do all Alaskans wear red suspenders?" Annie had wondered about that ever since she had arrived.

"Only if they want to keep their pants up," Robert replied, chuckling.

But Robert didn't let himself be diverted for long and he went back to his casting. Twice he got a strike, twice he fought the long silver-sided char, and twice he lost his prize. The second time, the char took off with his lure so that he had to rummage through his tackle box for another.

"That was my best lure, a Mepps four," he complained.

"That's too bad. That fish was really independent," Annie commented, still pleased with herself for the bear trick.

At least Robert didn't seem to hold a grudge. He put down his rod and stretched out beside her. "The word I'd use would be fighter, but independent fits too, I guess. Independence seems to be a way of life we all get used to up here. Man, I know when I'm in school, I get to feeling real closed in. All those classes and labs give me claustrophobia. Sometimes I have to take off for a while just to keep breathing."

"What year are you, Robert?" Annie ran her hand over a rounded cobblestone, washed smooth by centuries of flowing water.

"I have two years to go. I can't believe I've stuck it out this long. It's been hard." Robert's voice was pensive.

"Dad wants me to go to college. Stanford, like my sister and brother," Annie said, and without realizing it, sighed.

Robert looked over at her. "You don't sound very enthusiastic."

Annie shrugged. "I probably can't even get in Stanford. Besides, I'd rather work a year or two after high school . . . maybe not even go to college at all." Now why had she said that? She hadn't confided that to anyone, not even to her friend Lisa.

"What does your father say about that?"

"I haven't told him."

Robert raised his eyebrows in one continuous interested line that was a question without words.

"Dad is . . . it's just that Dad . . . I mean, it's hard to tell Dad anything he doesn't want to hear. He has a way of blocking it out like you never said it. It doesn't matter anyway. Dad's way usually works out best in the end." Annie had never before verbalized what had been a fact of her life for as long as she could remember, but it was true. Dad always did think he

61

knew what was best for everyone, and to be honest, he was usually right.

Robert started to tie a new lure onto his line. "You oughtta talk to Val."

"Val?"

"Val grew up in a Russian community of Old Believers who try to live the way people lived three hundred years ago. When the communists took over Russia, a whole lot of Old Believers left. They hate communism just about more than anything in the world. Anyway, for the next fifty years, they moved all over, and some of them ended up settling here in Alaska. You wouldn't believe how they live, strictly 17th-century stuff, no TV or booze or tobacco. It took Val three years to get up the guts to leave the community and make it on his own. When he gave up the old ways, his family disowned him."

So that's why Val had an accent and why he was so negative about the treaty with the Russians. But to be disowned by his family. Annie was horrified. "I couldn't ever do that. I couldn't manage without my family. I don't always agree with them, but I couldn't get along without them." The thought of cutting ties and leaving home forever was beyond Annie's comprehension. And to have her family angry at her would be unbearable.

One look at Annie's expression and Robert reached over, grabbed her hand and pulled her to her feet. "Come on, I'm going to show you how to fish whether you want to or not."

It's all in the wrist, Robert said as he stood behind Annie with his left hand gripping her left hand and his right hand holding her right wrist. As he guided her cast, Annie was very much aware of his muscular body pressed against hers. Maybe that was why she couldn't do it right until she finally moved away and tried it on her own. Actually, it wasn't as difficult as it looked, and after the first couple of attempts when she got her line all tangled up, she had a perfect cast. Whiiiippp. There, she had it, and it *was* in the wrist.

Now she was working downstream along the riverbank while Robert worked upstream. And then she felt that magic tug on her line, a tautness, the pull of a catch, and in the clear water, the flash of a bluish-green back. She had hooked a char. But landing it was a different story.

Robert was as excited as she was. "Keep the tip of your rod up . . . don't jerk your line . . . reel in slowly . . . don't let him get in the rocks . . . keep him in deep water . . ." But after a good five-minute fight, the line snapped and the char got away.

How many hours she and Robert fished, Annie had no idea and certainly the ever-present sun gave her no indication of the time. Robert caught three char, all over two feet long and weighing nine or ten pounds each. Annie finally landed a little one that couldn't have been more than seven pounds but she was as delighted as if it had weighed fifteen.

Suddenly there was a blast of wind and a roar of rotor blades above them. It was Lester in *Olyve Oil* dipping in salute as he flew over.

"Lester's on his way to pick up Glenn and Norman," Robert said. "We'd better get these fish up to the cook shack for dinner. One nice thing about Willy Lou, she doesn't mind gutting anything we catch." Robert laughed as he strung the four char on a forked stick, helped Annie gather up the fishing tackle and started toward camp.

They walked back to Little Salmon without talking. Annie was reflecting on her afternoon, the companionable silences she had shared with Robert, the incredible transparency of the river, the warmth of the sun in the limitless sky, the excitement of her catch. A satisfactory afternoon in every way. She and Robert parted with a wave, Robert to deliver the char and Annie to head for the bathhouse and a shower.

The shower water was good and hot and there seemed to be plenty of it. Annie washed her hair, then lingered until the water began to sputter and hiss before finally giving out. Taking her time, she dried off, combed out her hair and dressed. But as soon as she opened the bathhouse door, she was aware of loud shouting and yelling from down by the river. It was Val, running up the path toward her, his long face radiating alarm.

"Where's Mac?" Frantic. He kept on going without waiting for an answer.

Now Annie realized more people were approaching, a group of men slowly making their way up the path behind Val. One of them was Beers, Annie could see that, but she didn't recognize the others. There were three of them, all dressed in heavy winter clothes and wool caps. One had a ripped blanket wrapped around his shoulders and the tallest of the three held his left elbow with his right hand as if he had hurt it. They were unshaven and haggard looking, with wind-chapped faces and dark circled eyes.

Annie stood by the bathhouse staring at the men as they trudged up the path toward her. Beers followed, his pale face paler than ever and his brook-blue eyes blinking rapidly. The men were silent, their heads bowed in numbed exhaustion. Although they looked more bedraggled than menacing, Annie felt a sudden sense of foreboding. They're campers, that's all, or fishermen who have gotten lost, she told herself.

They didn't glance up as they trooped past her, but Beers paused. "Me and Val were working on the water pump when they came up to us. They're foreigners. I can't understand a word they say, but Val can and they told him they're defectors come over by fishing boat from Siberia . . . Russia. Can you believe it?" Beers' voice was shrill as he looked at Annie with a blank stare of astonishment on his thin face.

12

Val's panicked shout for Mac raised everyone in camp. Mac came running from the office shack, with Willy Lou and Robert appearing out of the cook shack. Then there was Annie, who didn't move. Russians. As implausible as it sounded, Annie realized it was possible. Everything about the three men, from their boots to their wool caps to their un-American–looking clothes communicated different, foreign, strange.

Now everyone was talking at once, with Val's voice rising above the others. "Defectors . . . Soviet Union . . ."

As Mac herded them all into the cook shack and they disappeared inside, Annie heard their excited voices blend into an unintelligible babble of sound. She knew there was no way she could retreat to her tent and close the door the way she wanted to, but she also knew that she would have to get her act together before she could face that cook shack full of people. She paused a long moment, sucked in her breath, straightened her shoulders and slowly, very slowly, headed up the path.

Everyone was gathered in a tense circle around the three men as Annie, not yet ready to commit herself to the situation, studied the group. There was Val, the focal point. She had never been able to figure out how old Val was and she couldn't now. With his long, gloomy face and curving lines that parenthesized his clean-shaven mouth, he could have been anywhere from twenty-two to thirty-five. Robert, who leaned forward intently, had pulled his jacket back to reveal his gun in an obvious power move. Willy Lou stood with both hands jammed on her wide hips, a ladle clutched in one hand like a weapon. Beers' mouth hung slackly open and his lashless eyes bulged like a befuddled goldfish. Mac, with his height, his full copper-red beard and red suspenders over a plaid wool shirt, dominated the group.

Slowly Annie edged up behind Willy Lou. Her broad back and strong work hands set on her hips meant business and Annie had more faith in the ladle still dripping gravy on the floor than in Robert's gun.

Now all three Russians were talking at once, directing their comments to Val, who kept shaking his head. "*Gavarite medlyenna. Gavarite medlyenna.* Speak slowly. Speak slowly."

The Russians seemed to understand. At least they nodded in some kind of agreement. Val turned to Mac. "All I know is archaic seventeenth-century Russian so I can't get what they say if they talk too fast. I told them to pick a leader." Val had a thin film of perspiration across his forehead and Annie noticed damp circles under his arms. She was so numbly cold, it was impossible to imagine anyone being able to sweat.

"Ivan Reutov, Josef Martushev, Grigory Kozhin." The oldest and shortest of the three seemed to be in charge as he pointed to each man in turn, with himself last. Although he was obviously introducing them, to Annie the names were just long syllables, meaningless nonsense words.

"They look frozen. How 'bout getting us all some coffee and something to eat, Willy Lou?" Mac asked without taking his eyes off the three men. "And you, Val, find out how they got here."

There was a long exchange in Russian, with hesitations, repeats, questions, consultations. Finally Val indicated the spokesman. "Grigory Kozhin here says they stole a fishing boat and set out from Naukan on the Siberian coast hoping to reach our coast at Wales. But their motor conked out and the currents picked them up. They don't know how long they were at sea, two or three days maybe, before they landed down where the Lanatak River flows into the Chukchi Sea. They saw one of our oil drums down there and figured they'd find a village in this direction. They've been following the Lanatak for two days, eating blueberries and what they could find along the way until they came on me and Beers fixing the water pump."

"What do they want?"

"Are there only three?"

"Shouldn't we frisk 'em?"

Everyone was talking at once, even Willy Lou, who had returned with coffee and a platter of thick cheese sandwiches.

Mac quieted them all down. "Ask why they're here. What do they want?" he ordered Val as Willy Lou passed the food and coffee.

This time the deliberations stretched out, five minutes, ten, as Val struggled with Grigory's too-rapid explanation. Now all three Russians were back in it, interrupting one another, making corrections, emphasizing a point. Annie was beginning to feel lightheaded and she was shaking with cold. Coffee, maybe coffee would help. But there were no more coffee cups on the tray. Everyone had coffee but her. She wasn't here, that's what. Of course, the whole thing was a dream and she as the dreamer had no part to play.

Now Grigory Kozhin took out a plastic map case from his coat pocket, opened it and pulled out official-looking blueprints, photographs, papers, maps. He spread them on the table and indicated different locations on the map to Val, with the other two Russians adding their own excited comments at the same time they were wolfing down the sandwiches and coffee.

Val, who was having a hard time keeping up, kept raising his hand to slow them down. His face was now visibly wet and he rubbed his palms on his blue jeans over and over as if to dry them. At last he turned to Mac. "It's . . . it's bad . . . we have to do something . . ."

Mac pounded his fist on the table. "My God, what is it?"

Val swallowed hard. "They say they have proof of a Soviet missile base in Siberia with nuclear warheads primed and set in violation of last year's agreement. All three of them have been working on the project . . ."

"Those missiles must be pointed right at us!" Beers' voice was as high-pitched as a child's.

Annie didn't hear that. Beers had never said it. But he had said it, she had heard it, and much as she wanted to stay detached, at that moment, she was sucked right into jeopardy with the rest of them.

"Let me finish," Val snapped, angry at Beers' interruption. "The Soviet premier doesn't even know the base exists. Their military, who were opposed to any kind of negotiations with the U.S. from the beginning, built it secretly. As soon as the Soviet premier signs the treaty in Geneva and returns to Moscow, the military are going to take the base out of wraps. Our satellites will pick it up on aerial photographs." Val paused to wipe his face with his red kerchief. "I think I got this right. I hope I got this right. The existence of the missile base will automatically void the treaty. The Soviet military are counting on world outcry to topple their government so they can stage a takeover."

There was a thunderstruck silence as everyone stared, first at Val and then at the three Russians.

"It's impossible. Are you sure you got it straight, Val?" Mac's voice wasn't much more than a whisper.

68

"Basically straight. And look at their maps and photographs. They seem authentic."

"I don't believe it. The whole thing's a trick." That was Willy Lou. Scornful.

"Maybe so, but how can we take the chance it isn't?" Mac had picked up one of the maps and was studying it. "Val, you're sure you know what you're talking about?"

Val nodded. "I went over it with them three times. And their papers look valid." Now Val dried both hands with his kerchief.

Mac placed the maps back on the table. "We can't risk not following through on this, but we have no radio. No way to get word out. Tell them."

For some reason Annie glanced over at Robert, who returned the look with all expression wiped clean from his face as if he had just found himself in the middle of an earthquake. Annie felt the same way, drained, in shock.

Val was translating Mac's message. Instantly the Russians protested in an explosion of alarm as Val strained to catch their words.

"They say they have to talk to American authorities immediately. By now they must be missed. They say they're vulnerable here and afraid."

Annie seized the words. Vulnerable. Afraid. But they were all vulnerable perched here on the edge of the continent, like those ancient pictures of ships toppling over the flat corners of the earth. And there was no need for Val to say the men were afraid. They exuded fear. Annie could always smell it. She was exuding the same smell of fear herself.

13

Mac took a deep breath. "Okay, Val, tell them we got a helicopter out in the field that's due back in . . . let's see . . . Norman and Glenn went out about sixty-five miles today . . . due back in about an hour and a half. As soon as Lester refuels, we'll fly the men to Kotz."

As Val translated, Mac lit up a cigar and took a frustrated puff. "What a summer," he said to no one in particular. "Everything's gone wrong that could possibly go wrong and now I'm stuck with this on my hands and no radio."

Grigory Kozhin had grabbed Val's arm and was talking fast, his face lined with concern. Val listened, nodding. "They say an hour and a half is too long," Val repeated. "Certainly they have been missed and a search has been launched. Can't anything else be done?"

"Not unless they want to walk." Mac's cigar bobbed up and down as he talked. "But while we wait, we can go over their papers and maps with them." Mac took out his cigar and jabbed it in the air. "You, Beers, find these men some clothes. They're about your size, no, Glenn's size. Anybody's size. Just get them something warm to put on, and hurry. Willy Lou, rustle up more chow and coffee. Hot. Get us all fed. Val, you and the men come with me to the office shack where it's quiet. The two of us will fly to Kotz with them, you to translate and me on principle."

Willy Lou didn't budge. "I can't make more coffee. The water pump's broke again, Mac."

Mac's florid face reddened all the way up over his baldness. "Didn't you and Beers get that fixed this afternoon, Val?"

Val shook his head. "It was working okay, then went sour on us."

The more excited Mac got, the larger he loomed, almost as if he were swelling. "Robert, see what you can do with the pump. I need Val with me."

"Yeah, I'll try," Robert answered and with that, everyone scattered, intent, purposeful, the pale look of uncertainty gone from their faces. Everyone but Annie. No one had asked her to do anything. It was just as well. She didn't feel capable of functioning on even a fundamental level.

And she had to get fresh air. Pressure had been building up in her lungs and now it was so excruciating, she could hardly breathe. She stepped outside, closed her eyes, and inhaled the cool damp air into her suffocating lungs. Although she hadn't consciously been thinking of home, the moment she shut her eyes, she saw her mother bustling around the kitchen fixing breakfast and getting ready for work at the same time, with Scott pumping iron in his room with his usual grunts and groans, and Dad slamming the front door as he came in from his morning jog.

The scene was so vivid that when Annie opened her eyes and saw the late afternoon sun clinging to the horizon, the rounded peaks of somber gray mountains patched with snow, the miles and miles of open plains, she felt a physical stab. Barren ground. It was barren ground all right, a good name.

71

Slowly Annie turned and headed for her tent to get her parka. She was cold clear through to the core of her.

"Hey, Short Straw."

It was Beers. He stood by Glenn and Norman's tent waving something. With a job to do, even Beers looked more like his old self.

"I brought this wrench back with me by mistake. Take it down to Robert, willya?"

At last someone had noticed her and given her a job. Annie took the wrench from Beers, ran into her tent, snatched up her parka, then raced down the path toward the river. Hey, she was able to function after all.

When she reached the riverbank, she found Robert already working on the dismantled pump. Pulled up high on the rocky shore nearby was what must have been the mud tub, a galvanized tub about six feet long, three feet wide and three feet deep with two homemade paddles shoved under two wooden slats that served as seats. USS *Foxy* was painted on the stern.

Annie hunkered down next to Robert. "Here's your wrench."

"Hey, now we're getting somewhere. Thanks, Short." Robert looked up and smiled and when Annie saw that disarming grin spread across his face, she couldn't help smiling back.

"Stay here and talk to me while I work."

Yes, right now that was what Annie wanted too. She couldn't face camp, where everyone was running around like crazy and those Russians were there with their terrifying maps and papers and documents. She sat down close to Robert and watched the river bubble and murmur on its crystal passage to the sea. The two ducks she had seen the evening she had arrived were back, resting on a rock.

Annie pointed to them. "What kind of ducks are those, Robert?"

Robert looked up. "Harlequin. They're neat, aren't they?"

With white round clown spots behind their eyes and white masks over their faces, they certainly looked like harlequins. Annie watched them until the male squawked and they flew away.

Robert broke the silence. "What were you thinking about back there in the cook shack?" he asked without looking up.

Annie studied his face in profile and again noticed the bump on his nose that wasn't visible from the front. "I wished Dad was here." Her answer surprised her. Although it had just popped out, as soon as she said it, she knew it was true. If she couldn't be home, then she wished her father was here. Annie couldn't ever remember a situation that Dad couldn't handle.

Robert seemed to understand what she meant. "Mac is okay. He gets uptight and excited, but it doesn't last. And he's a competent guy."

Maybe. But Annie didn't want to talk about Mac. "I . . . I . . . was thinking about a whole lot else too . . ." she hesitated. She had been thinking about the unthinkable, the horror of that mushroom cloud becoming a reality.

"So was I." Robert sounded wistful. "I was thinking maybe I won't ever finish college and come back here to Alaska as a geologist. I was thinking about the draft and the army and war. I never believed it could happen, but all of a sudden, it's a possibility." Robert's eyes had an unfocused faraway look and there was another silence between them.

Annie looked down at her red hands. They were wrinkly and chapped and all her nails were broken, almost like an old woman's and it suddenly occurred to her that she might never live to be an old woman. She rubbed her hands together as if to bring them to life, then unzipped her parka. Although the sun was low, she could feel its warmth and that suffocating pressure was beginning to build up in her chest again.

"My sister and brother are into the nuclear protest movement in a big way so they talk about it all the time and they get lots of pamphlets and magazines in the mail," she began slowly. "I don't want to listen to them or look at their stuff, but I do. I read all the horror stories and statistics and now it's like they're all coming true. I guess I'm worried that I'll never have the chance to grow old."

Robert didn't say anything. He just put down his wrench, slid over close to Annie and put his arms around her. Her arms went around him too, and for a long moment, he held her that way, stroking her hair as if he were comforting a child. Then he took her chin in his hand and tipped it up so she was looking into his dark eyes. His nose and mouth and mustache came closer and closer until his lips pressed against hers, gently at first, and then more insistently. And she was kissing him back, his prickly mustache brushing her face in a not unpleasant way. The rhythm of her heart picked up and she wasn't sure if it was her heartbeat she felt through her sweater or Robert's. He drew back and smiled down at her.

"Ah, Short Straw, you're not such a little girl after all," he said and then he kissed her hard, parting her lips.

It wiped out everything. Annie couldn't think of anything but Robert's lips on hers and his body pressed against her body and for the moment it was enough. Then Robert gave her a hard hug, a quick kiss on the cleft in her chin and pulled away. He was still smiling, his teeth startling white against his dark mustache.

"I'd better get going on this or Mac will have my head," he said as he picked up his wrench.

The remark snapped Annie back to reality. They were insane to be down here making out when their world was about to blow apart. She tried to be angry, but she could still feel Robert's arms around her and it was too mellow a memory for anger. She hugged her knees and watched a line of caribou move across a gray talus slope in the distance. Now the pump was sputtering and whirring and Robert was reconnecting everything up.

74

"Not a bad job." Robert sounded pleased with himself as he began to gather up his tools.

"If only . . ."

"Sh." Robert cocked his head to one side. "Do you hear that?"

The gurgling river, the whirring pump, a little vole scooting across the stones on tiny scratchy feet. And something else. The sound of a motor . . .

"It must be Lester coming back from the field with Norman and Glenn," Annie said. Good, Lester could take those Russians and fly them out of here forever.

Robert shook his head. "That's not *Olyve Oil*."

At his somber tone of voice, Annie's head jerked up. "What is it then?"

Now the motor was louder, coming closer.

"It sounds like a helicopter, but I can't tell what direction it's coming from." Robert was on his feet, the ridiculous baseball cap on the back of his head a contrast to his grim expression. Something was wrong. Slowly Annie got to her feet too. And then she could feel it, a thumping vibration that filled the air, shook the ground, and invaded her body with its beat. Now she could see it too, a huge helicopter, flying from the west toward them, flying so low it barely skimmed over the mountains.

"Quick, Short, follow me." Robert grabbed his tools, threw them in the tool box, and charged down the gravel riverbank as fast as he could. He ran about one hundred feet, then followed a game trail that cut through the brush. He darted around a turn in the trail and was instantly out of sight. Now the helicopter was close enough for Annie to see it was dark green, with big white numbers painted over.

Then Annie was running down the gravel bank too, until she found the cut in the brush where Robert had disappeared. Ducking low, she followed the trail until she came on Robert, crouched beneath some low-lying branches. He reached up, took her hand and pulled her down beside him. There was no way the short run justified the way her legs folded up under her.

"A military chopper . . . camouflaged . . . coming from the coast low enough to avoid radar. Soviet aircraft. It must be a Soviet aircraft." Robert sounded breathless, and when Annie looked at him, she saw her own alarm reflected on his stricken face.

14

$\mathbf{N}$ow the air was devoured by the beat of the blades and the roar of the engine. Annie was rigid, all scrunched up with her arms over her head, not able to see and wishing she couldn't hear. Robert, crouched beside her, was just as tense. She could feel the hard muscles of his arm and leg wedged against hers.

The helicopter was landing. The whine of the blades changed, shifted, and even here sheltered by the dense thicket, the blast of the wind swept through their hiding place. Almost immediately there was the sound of male voices yelling something incomprehensible, barked commands, running boots, all drowning out the murmur of the Lanatak River.

"A foreign language . . . Russian . . . it's gotta be Russians come for the defectors." Robert whispered so close to Annie's ear she flinched from the tickle of his mustache.

From camp there were more shouts, orders being given, men running. A sudden blast of gunshot. Instant silence. Willy Lou, Mac, Beers, Val, the defectors. One by one Annie pictured them. She had tears in her eyes and didn't know it until she looked at Robert and they spilled over. Her expression pleaded with him to assure her that no one was hurt.

77

Robert pressed her hand. "They must be rounding everyone up. That was just a warning shot, I'm sure." Robert's voice was as strained as his face. He had to control his own panic so Annie wouldn't give in to hers.

Another shout. This time Annie recognized Val's voice, calling out something in Russian and the sounds that followed were more low-key, not so frenzied, a shout here and there, but no more gunshots. Please, Annie prayed, no more gunshots.

"What should we do?" she gasped.

Robert put his other arm around her shoulder. "Nothing. We're safe here for now."

But they weren't safe. The Russians had landed at Little Salmon. With guns. And there was no way they could be safe hiding in this brush when Robert himself had said it was bear habitat. There was no such thing as safe.

The noise and confusion from camp quieted down, with only an occasional shout or door slamming. Annie's jaw ached from clenching her teeth, and although Robert's arm across her shoulders was a dead weight, she didn't want him to move it. His arm was all that was preventing her from jumping up and yelling her head off. No, Robert's arm was essential. And then his arm was gone and she could feel his body pull away.

"I'm going to try and see what's going on. Stay here. I'll be right back."

Annie reached out and grabbed his sleeve. "Don't go," she begged. "Please don't leave me."

Robert took hold of her hand, released his sleeve from her grip and forced her to look into his eyes. "I have to find out what's happening. Don't move or make a sound. Do you understand?" Although Robert was whispering, his tone left no room for argument.

Numbly Annie nodded.

Every step Robert took out of the brush sounded like a

78

firecracker exploding as twigs snapped underfoot. As soon as he was gone, Annie decided she would give him ten minutes and if he didn't come back, she'd go after him. I won't look at my watch for five minutes, she promised herself. But when she had waited for what must surely have been the full ten minutes, only three and a half minutes had passed. Her watch must be broken. She held it up to her ear. No, it was still running.

The Russians had seen Robert. They had killed him. They had killed everyone else too. She was the only one left. Alone. Bear bait. Annie whipped herself into such a state that when she heard a twig break, she jumped up, cracking her head on a low branch.

It was Robert. But all the blood had rushed from Annie's head and his face blurred in a whirl of vertigo. Robert, who was breathless and panting himself, didn't notice.

"As far as I can tell, everyone, including the defectors, are okay," he whispered. "They're all in the office shack under guard. They're Russians, all right, about fifteen men, with half of 'em out searching camp, probably to make sure they didn't miss anyone." Robert took off his cap and ran his fingers through his hair.

"Don't talk . . ." he muttered, ". . . let me think . . . they don't know we're here yet . . . they'll find out soon enough from the camp roster that I'm missing . . ."

Robert didn't have to worry about Annie talking. She didn't have one coherent thought in her head, not what to say, where to go, what their next move should be. She was totally disconnected, waiting for Robert to tell her what to do.

"We have to get outta here . . . later, when it's dark . . ." Robert's chest was still heaving in and out as he looked at Annie and studied her face, deliberating, calculating. "It's okay, Short . . . we'll make it . . . you and I together . . ."

There it was, the reassurance that Annie needed. Robert's

in-charge expression with his eyebrows pulled together in a determined line plainly communicated that he was on top of the situation. With a sense of relief, Annie wiggled around to get into a more comfortable position. Her jeans were damp clear through and her back ached from being all cramped up.

Neither of them spoke. Robert was obviously so deep in thought he didn't want to talk, and Annie couldn't think of anything to say. Besides, they didn't dare risk being overheard. In the silence, it was Annie who heard the motor first, a distinct thumping beat in the air, a helicopter and no question about it. More helicopters. More power moves. More guns.

Now Robert heard it too. He listened a moment, then turned to Annie. "It's Lester, bringing back Norman and Glenn from the field. I'd recognize *Olyve Oil* anywhere."

Lester! Annie had forgotten all about him. Why, Lester could save them. As soon as he saw the Russian helicopter at Little Salmon, he'd keep going and get help.

Apparently Lester had no such plans. The blades changed pitch and *Olyve Oil* landed. As soon as the motor cut off and the blades stopped racketing, the harsh foreign voices barked out again. At least there were no gunshots, only a surprised, "Hey, what's going on?" from Norman, followed by more words, some American, indignant and protesting, and some Soviet, sharp and authoritative. Annie wondered if Lester's stoical expression changed, or whether he just kept chewing away on his tobacco with his eyes masked by those reflective dark glasses. Lester and *Olyve Oil*, their only chance down the tubes.

Robert must have known what she was thinking. "Lester never was a possibility. He had a long flight out to pick up Glenn and Norman and had to be real short on fuel. And if he'd tried to get away, the Russians could have shot him down easy."

Annie hadn't thought of that, but of course, Robert was

right. Lester and Norman and Glenn were probably already being hustled off to the office shack with the others. All of a sudden, the office shack didn't seem like such a bad idea. At least everyone would be there, especially Willy Lou with her low-key warmth and there would be consolation in that.

"Maybe we should give ourselves up, Robert."

Robert's head jerked around and he stared at Annie as if she'd just suggested treason. "Are you crazy?"

"But we can't hide here forever."

"You're right. We can't. We've got to get word out. As I see it, if our satellites show up that Russian missile base after the treaty is signed, everyone will say these defectors are just a put-up Commie job to get their government off the hook. Which means we've got to do something about it now."

As far as Robert was concerned, that apparently was that. Unfortunately, Annie could also see that somehow, in some way, Robert was including her in that "we," and she wasn't sure she wanted to know what he had in mind.

Like it or not, Robert laid it out for her. "I figure we'll stay here until dark, then paddle the mud tub downstream a ways and then head out for Niyuk. We can call for help on Niyuk's satellite phone hookup."

Annie's face went slack. So this was Robert's big decision and the "we" meant he assumed she was going. No way. The thought of setting out on the river at night in a flimsy little metal tub rated about zero on Annie's scale of one to ten. If Robert wanted to go on his own, that was fine. She would give herself up. After all, she couldn't be any worse off in the office shack than she would be going along with that crazy scheme.

15

Saying no to Robert wasn't easy. Robert was determined to carry out his plan and insisted that he couldn't control the tub on his own, that he had to have Annie's help. Even when Annie said she knew nothing about paddling or canoes or tubs, he pressed. And Robert was very good at pressing. On the other hand, Annie was very good at keeping still. She simply shut her mouth and wouldn't speak until Robert finally gave up arguing.

The mosquitoes were enough to keep them busy anyway. Dad had said the mosquito season was over, but no one had told the mosquitoes, and they whined and attacked from every direction, making it almost impossible to concentrate on anything else. Gradually, despite their discomfort, the sky turned golden, that special half-light that hushed everything into an amber glow, and the mosquitoes began to calm down.

But that wasn't the end of the interlopers. Annie had just shifted into a more comfortable position when there was a crashing in the brush behind her. A huge porcupine, at least three feet long and bristling with quills, was lumbering through the willows not six feet away. With its awkward chunky body and short stubby legs, it wasn't making any kind of time, but at the sight of it, Annie threw herself at Robert.

Startled by the commotion, the porcupine immediately raised its quills, turned around and switched its tail back and forth. Annie covered her face with her hands and braced herself for a bombardment of the vicious-looking barbs. Nothing happened. There was a moment of silence and then a loud thrashing noise and snapping of twigs as the porcupine waddled off, leaving Robert choked with laughter.

"He tried to throw his quills at me." Annie's words were almost a sob.

Robert was still laughing. "Porkies can't throw quills. They can only release them if you brush against them. A porky is the dumbest, clumsiest animal around."

Dumb and clumsy or not, the porcupine was one fright too many. "I'm going to give myself up, Robert. I can't stand it here another minute."

Before she could move, Robert seized her arm. "I need you, Short. I can't get to Niyuk without your help. And remember what you said about wondering if you'd ever grow old? Think about it. If you want that option, then you'd better take your chances with me."

Robert's grip on her arm was urgent, and for the first time, Annie was forced to consider the alternatives. There were plenty of people who had argued against a disarmament treaty with the Russians from the beginning, and when those American satellite photographs revealed a secret Soviet missile base in Siberia, it would give them all the evidence they needed to prove that the Russians couldn't be trusted. And as Robert said, no one would believe the defectors weren't anything but a put-up Soviet job.

For sure, the uproar that would follow would ruin any future negotiations, and the horrors would begin all over again, arms build-up, nuclear stockpiling, development of new warheads. And if the military took over the Soviet government, there might even be war. Those were the alternatives and Annie didn't want them. On the other hand, she couldn't bring herself to make a commitment to Robert either.

"I don't know, Robert . . . it's too heavy . . . I can't handle it . . ."

"You've got until dark to decide, Short, and this time you're going to have to make up your own mind." Robert wasn't pressuring anymore. In fact, his low voice sounded almost sympathetic, as if he felt sorry for her. Maybe he did, because he stretched out his legs, worked the kinks out of his shoulders and reached over and pulled Annie close to him in a gesture of protection and caring.

"Some day, Short, you're going to have to stand up and be counted, and maybe this is the time. You know . . ." Abruptly Robert snatched his arm away and sat bolt upright.

"What is it?"

Muffled voices. Sounds of people approaching. Suddenly Annie was cold, terribly cold as Robert yanked her tight against him, the insistence of his arm warning her to be quiet, not to make a sound. Male footsteps clumped over nearby rocks, and curt voices spoke brusquely, unintelligibly. There was a question here, a terse reply there, another short foreign burst of words as boots tramped by their hiding place.

Those men just beyond the thicket were the ultimate reality. Without even putting the thought into words, way in the back of her mind, Annie had harbored the possibility that this whole crisis was a hoax, some sort of macabre game. But there was no denying the rough voices or the heavy-booted footsteps. Russians were here at Little Salmon Camp, searching for her, Ann Jamison Sloane. With guns. She didn't have to see the guns to know that they were there. Robert had said his people believed that grizzlies could sense the presence of a gun, and Annie could too.

In the end, it was those alien voices that convinced Annie to go with Robert. There was no way she could give herself up to those voices. Her eyes met Robert's and he knew without words what her decision would be. But it was a long wait until dark. The golden light lingered as the sun set unwillingly. Although Annie had vowed not to sleep, curled up against Robert's warmth, she dozed, never fully asleep, but not completely awake either. She drifted from awareness of the river sounds and purring of the water pump, to nebulous dreams of home and family and safety.

And then, at the realization that Robert was easing his arm out from under her, Annie was instantly alert. The moon was out bright in a dark sky, a vivid silver ball glowing with an almost fluorescent radiance. In the narrow space between them, Robert fixed Annie with a hard stare.

"I want you to do exactly what I say and don't ask questions," he whispered. "Now follow me."

Without waiting for her response, Robert got up and held back the tangle of branches for Annie to follow. But Annie could hardly move. She had a cramp in one leg and her back felt as twisted as the stunted willows. Even when they reached the gravel riverbank, she found it hard to straighten up, and although Robert looked just as uncomfortable, he didn't hesitate.

"Okay, Short, help me carry the tub down to the water."

There was that terrible effort to move, but with every step, muscles and tendons eased a little and the tub wasn't as heavy as it looked. When they were almost to the water's edge, Robert took out the paddles and laid them on the ground. "Turn the tub over," he ordered.

Obediently, Annie swung her end up and over in unison with Robert, then waited for her next directions like a child.

"I want you to wait for me under this tub. You'll be safer here than anywhere," Robert said. "I'm going to camp and I won't be gone long. The minute I get back, we're gonna take off down the river. Understand?"

"But . . ."

Robert didn't give Annie time to argue. He simply lifted up one end of the overturned tub and gestured for her to crawl in. As soon as Annie was under the tub, Robert brought it back down over her. The moonlight was instantly cut off and she was surrounded by an echoey kind of darkness. Robert knocked on the tub's bottom and it resounded through her head with a tinny reverberation.

"Stay cool, Short. I'll be back soon."

Annie scrunched under the tub hugging herself for warmth and protection. Being totally enclosed by metal exaggerated the night noises, the splash of the water, the on-and-off whir of the water pump, a distant owl, the scurry of little animals, the wind rustling through the willow leaves. This couldn't be happening. Hiding under a mud tub, in the middle of the night, putting her life in the hands of someone she hardly knew. She should have stood up for herself, told Robert he couldn't leave her, or even insisted that she go with him.

The mud tub wasn't even that safe a shelter. A curious bear could easily tip it over, and in the bright moonlight, she'd be as exposed as a bug under an overturned rock. What was Robert doing anyway? He said he was going back to camp, but why? Turn himself over to the Russians . . . hold them up with his gun . . . free the crew . . . take off in the helicopter without her . . . No, she was going off the deep end. He wouldn't leave her behind. He couldn't, not when he had promised to come back.

Annie was so still, it was as if she were rooted in time and space. An animal scratched at the tub and it sounded as loud as a clanging cymbal. A silent scream circled in her chest. A bear, raking its three-inch unretractable claws across the metal. But there was a familiar low-pitched cry, and Annie realized it was a porcupine, probably the one they'd seen earlier, not that that fact was very reassuring. She was almost hyperventilating now. The hard seats of the mud tub pressed into her back. Her neck was stiff and sore . . .

"Annie, it's me, Robert."

It was an urgent hiss close to her ear and a sharp tap on the side of the tub. Annie was so startled that she jumped up, forgetting where she was, and smacked her head. Now the tub was being lifted off her. She blinked in the white moonlight.

"Get up. Hurry." Robert leaned down, grabbed her arm and pulled her to her feet. Now he jammed his face so close to hers all she could see were his dark eyes.

"Get the tub into the water. Fast!" Robert released his grip on her arm as he threw two backpacks into the tub, tossed in the paddles and grabbed one end of the tub, signaling Annie to take the other.

There was no argument. No discussion. The decision was taken out of Annie's hands as they dropped the tub into the water. Robert held it steady for Annie to get in, then jumped in the stern and pushed off with one of the paddles. The tub scraped over the rocks, then the current picked them up and they were launched.

Va-Room!

A violent explosion ripped the night apart. Dumbfounded, Annie leapt up, but the tub rocked so precariously she immediately fell back on her seat again. Behind them, at camp, a ball of fire shot into the air with a roar. It was the holocaust, everything that Annie had ever feared.

"Keep paddling!" Robert shouted.

Va-Room!

Another explosion as loud as the first threw more flames into the sky. The night had gone from silver-spangled stars to a crackling, snapping inferno.

"Don't stop. Paddle!" Robert yelled. "I did it. I set a fuse on

87

both choppers and blew them up. Now hurry, we gotta get out of here."

Robert's words washed over Annie as she dipped her paddle into the river. But her arms had turned rubbery and the paddle wobbled around uselessly.

"We have to make that turn up ahead. Faster!" Robert was still shouting.

Sa-whing!

Something sizzled past Annie, a whistling ping and although she had never heard it before, she knew right away what it was. A bullet. They were being shot at!

"Duck!"

Robert didn't need to say anything. Annie was already crouched down, almost flat out in the tub, the paddle clutched to her chest like a lifeline.

Sa-whing!

Now, in the swift water, the tub was careening around, spinning out of control, with Robert paddling furiously in the stern. Then, under his guidance, the tub straightened out, righted itself, and in moments they were around the bend in the river and out of sight.

16

Combined with that line of light that always seems to hover on the Arctic horizon, the moon shone bright enough to see by, with a million stars sprinkled overhead in a black, upside-down bowl. As the river carried Annie and Robert west, a ridge of low mountains cut off any view of the camp behind them except for a brilliant orange blush that silhouetted the dark peaks. The river was swift here, whitecapped, and the tub seemed to have a mind of its own as Robert fought to keep its bow pointed straight ahead. Over and over the tub swung sideways as Robert yelled at Annie to dig in and paddle. But it was hard for Annie to concentrate on paddling. Even though Robert had destroyed the helicopters, the Russians could have found another mud tub and followed them down the river, or started out after them on foot. Those bullets whistling past were a sound that Annie would never forget.

"Robert, are there other mud tubs at camp?" she called back.

Robert knew right away what was on her mind. "Only at the drill site, about fifteen miles upstream. Believe me, it's not worth the walk to get one, and besides, they wouldn't even know where to find them."

Good. Annie relaxed somewhat, although as they continued on their way westward, she was becoming increasingly colder. The near-freezing temperature of the water refrigerated the tub's metal bottom and from there, the cold penetrated through her boots into her feet and legs. Her breath came in little white puffs as she paddled harder and harder to keep her blood circulating.

"Hey, not so frantic," Robert yelled. "You'll tip us over."

Tipping over was the last thing Annie wanted. In the moonlight, the river looked inky black and bottomless, with little whitecaps of silver breaking the surface like peaks on a cake frosting. If water froze at 32°, this water must be 32½°.

Annie was concentrating so hard on sitting in the middle of her seat so as not to tip the tub, she didn't notice the rock jutting up in the middle of the river until there was a terrible grinding crunch. The tub came to a jarring stop that swung them around 90° and brought a loud groan from Robert.

"If the tub is punctured, we've had it." It was a mutter under his breath, but loud enough for Annie to hear, as he reached down and ran his hands along the bottom of the tub. There was a long indentation where the rock had dented the metal, but no water was leaking in. Robert's sigh of relief was audible.

"If you get your weight back here in the stern with me, Short, I think I can push us off."

Annie cautiously swung her legs over her seat and even more cautiously made her way to the stern all bent over, with her hands on the tub's gunnels. She knelt in a tight little ball, her arms hugging her chest so as to stay out of Robert's way. Robert braced his paddle on a nearby rock, and after a good deal of grunting and pushing, there was a rasping scrape and they were free, bobbing and turning in the water.

Back in the bow, Annie picked up her paddle, trying to keep everything straight, paddle hard but not too hard, sit in the middle and watch for rocks, as well as occasionally blowing on her hands so they wouldn't congeal from frostbite.

Then, between one moment and the next, the strip of light sky widened and the horizon to the northeast turned the soft pink of dawn. Only a few hours before the sunset had been these same rosy hues. A flick of an eye and the Arctic night was over. Although Annie saw no sign yet of the sun, its presence was already evident as the dark water began to blue up, and the cheeps and squawks and chirpings of birds sounded everywhere.

As they paddled along an easy stretch in that half-light between night and day, Annie noticed a quick movement on the riverbank and when she looked over, she saw a squat, heavy-bodied animal dart out of the brush twenty-five feet away. It looked something like a weasel but was more heavily furred and larger, about three or four feet long. It stood on its hind legs for a moment, its glittery eyes riveted on them before it stole back into the brush.

Robert had seen it too. "A wolverine," he called. "Lester says there's a pair living around here, but they're antisocial and I've never seen 'em."

Annie shuddered. Dad had told her that wolverines were so vicious they could tear down a caribou and even grizzlies didn't mess with them. She just hoped they were sufficiently antisocial that she never saw another.

The change from night to day was so gradual, it was hard to pinpoint when it happened, but all of a sudden, Annie realized that the sun had edged over the horizon and it was daylight. She didn't know whether to be relieved to see the sun in anticipation of its warmth, or whether it meant they could be spotted more easily if the Russians had found a way to follow them. Another Soviet helicopter or plane had come over, maybe, or they had constructed some kind of a raft to float down the river.

Annie rested her paddle and turned around. "What do you think, Robert, can the Russians follow us?"

Robert snorted. "No way. What are they gonna do, swim?"

Annie didn't answer. Even if Robert were lying to reassure her, she felt better. Besides, at this point, what could she do about it? For now, she'd just try to put it out of her mind.

It was turning out to be a beautiful day. The river, shimmering like new, had lightened to an incredible sapphire blue, and with each stroke, her paddle raised a necklace of sparkling diamonds.

"How deep is the water here?" she called back.

"About fifteen feet."

Fifteen feet, and yet Annie could see each individual rock on the bottom as if it were close enough to touch. She leaned over and let her fingers trail in the frigid water. They were in an open wide stretch, with enough current to keep them going, but without any of the earlier white water. In the distance a golden eagle soared high above them on the air currents, and it seemed impossible that it could sight prey on the ground below. Huge, black, raucous ravens stalked the riverbanks or took flight on wings that must have been close to four feet wide. Little animals darted and scurried in and out of the brush.

The sky was bright azure now, with not a cloud to be seen, as the sun continued to rise over the distant mountains, at last warming up the day. Although the land beside the river was low at times so that Annie had a long-range view of the countryside, most of the time, the river was banked with such high growth it was impossible to see beyond it. Protected and contained in the tub as it was swept along, Annie, for the first time, the very first time, didn't feel overwhelmed by the country, silenced by it, powerless.

There was a nudge at her back. Robert had poked her with his paddle and was pointing to something on the bank, a

92

caribou, poised on a ledge about ten feet above them, looking down. It was a bull, with a great arching rack of antlers and a long white beard below its massive neck. As Annie stared into its soft eyes, it seemed to stare back. An abrupt turn in the river and the caribou was out of sight.

Annie could hear Robert's laugh above the splash of the water. "It's my theory that moose and caribou get bored and are curious. He's probably wondering who we think we are messing around with his river."

Annie laughed too. It was true. And with its head cocked to one side that way, it looked something like old Mrs. Kenny their neighbor back home who watched everyone's comings and goings from behind her front window.

"I like to hear you laugh, Short," Robert called out.

Annie turned to glance back at him. He had peeled down to his shirt and his sleeves were rolled up. His arms were covered with fine, black hairs, with the blue veins prominent and his muscles tensing with each stroke of his paddle. What wonderful arms, she thought, then she realized that Robert was watching her watch him. A spark would be too romantic a word for what passed between them, but it was as strong as the rush of the water carrying them along and Annie remembered how those arms had held her.

Robert grinned. "You're doing real good, Short."

Don't call me that, Annie wanted to say. It made her feel small and insignificant, the old Runt-of-the-Litter syndrome again. But this wasn't the time to get into that, so she turned around and started paddling again, warmed by their exchange.

They traveled on, the river at times calm and peaceful and at other times peppered with rocks. Although they were swept up once in white water that was so swift they spun out of control, for the most part, their progress was steady as their little tub was carried down the twisting, winding Lanatak. As the day advanced, from morning to noon, and noon to afternoon, Annie tried to ignore her increasingly full kidneys and her increasingly empty stomach. Her hands were sore and blistered too, but she couldn't bear to think about stopping. The mud tub and the river were all.

But Robert had his own ideas. "We're going to land over on that bank, Short." He indicated the spot with his paddle.

No, not yet. Although the tub was Annie's secure haven, Robert was already guiding them toward shore. He leapt out into the shallow water, grabbed the bow and pulled it over the rocks. With her paddle clasped in her lap, Annie sat in the bow, unmoving.

"Get out, willya?" Robert directed. "I want to hide the tub in the brush so it can't be seen. We'll rest, get something to eat, maybe a fish if I can catch one, and then head out across the tundra to Niyuk."

Head out across the tundra? But that couldn't be. Robert hadn't said anything about crossing the tundra. Annie shook her head feebly. The tundra was exposed in every direction so they could be spotted easily by anyone following them, especially from the air, and . . . and . . . the tundra had other dangers, formidable, unpredictable dangers that had reigned here in the Arctic long before any two-footed intruders had come along.

17

At least the underbrush where Robert and Annie left the river was low and not terribly dense and for that Annie was grateful. Nothing ominous could hide in it or lurk behind it without being seen instantly. As soon as they landed, Robert asked for Annie's help in hiding the mud tub in the brush. If it had been up to Annie, she would have left the tub in plain sight in the hopes that someone would see it, be curious, and check it out with Little Salmon Camp.

Robert wasn't willing to take that chance. Now, for the first time, he acknowledged that it was possible they could have been followed. A back-up Soviet helicopter, or maybe a patrol sent out after them could conceivably be a problem. After all, the Russians must have maps of the area and realize that Niyuk, the closest settlement, was their probable destination. Robert's admission that he was worried didn't do much for Annie's morale, but it at least convinced her they should hide the tub.

Robert picked up the two paddles and stowed them under the seats. "Get the packs out, will you?"

Two worn backpacks lay in the bottom of the tub. When

Annie picked them up, she felt their full weight. "Where did these come from?"

"They're Glenn's and Norman's. I got them out of *Olyve Oil* before I set the fuses." Robert looked up with an expression of astonishment. "Hey, Short, did you hear that? I blew those choppers right off the face of the earth. I pulled it off, me, Robert Harry." Robert reached out for Annie, grabbed her around the waist and lifted her off her feet. "I did it. I really did it," he crowed as he whirled her around.

"Yeah, I know, Robert. It was great, but put me down, will you? I'm getting dizzy."

Robert gave her a hard hug and set her on her feet. "You know," he said, suddenly serious, "there's one thing I can't figure out. Why didn't the Russians just mow everyone down as soon as they landed?"

Mow everyone down? But that would have included Robert and her, too, if they'd been caught. They still might be caught. Maybe Robert had forgotten those bullets that had whizzed past them on the river, but Annie hadn't.

As Robert picked up one end of the mud tub and signaled Annie to grab hold of the other, he answered his own question. "They probably had orders to get the defectors back to Russia alive. Flying under our radar is tricky and they must have been waiting to take off until just before dawn when it's darkest. But what were they going to do with the Little Salmon crew?"

By now Robert had led Annie over to the heaviest stand of willows where he pulled aside the twisted branches and with Annie's help, shoved the mud tub deep into the brush until it was totally hidden.

"Were they going to kill the crew? Real risky. Let them go? Risky, too. Fly everyone back to Russia? That would make more problems than it would solve. Maybe they needed some kind of information from them. One thing for sure, they're not going anywhere now." All the time Robert had been talking, he had been poking around the brush looking for something. Now he came back with a long stick.

"Check through the backpacks, will you, Short, and see what Glenn and Norman left us to eat," he suggested. "I'm going to try and catch us some fish."

As Robert headed down the riverbank toward a big rock that was half submerged in the water, Annie opened the blue pack. It was obviously Glenn's. She recognized his wool fisherman cap and the pouch of tobacco that he carried for his pipe. But it was the food that Annie was interested in, a Hershey bar, half a bologna sandwich, and a bag of potato chips left over from lunch. The rest of the pack was filled with matches, a space blanket, an extra sweater, rain gear, a compass, knife, toilet paper.

The other pack, Norman's, held the usual field equipment as well as an apple and a stale roll of Life Savers that was all linty. Annie, with a glance toward Robert to make sure he wasn't looking, popped two Life Savers in her mouth, and although they were gummy soft, they helped ease her hunger pangs.

"Say, Robert . . ."

"Shhhh." Robert's shush was soft and drawn out, perfectly tuned to the rush and murmur of the moving water. He had already put together some kind of fishing pole and line and was kneeling on the rock, holding the pole out over the water.

Being quiet was fine with Annie. She sank down on the riverbank and with the warm sun on her face, watched the river flow by through thoughtful eyes. Crazy, this whole trip was crazy. If the Russian military wanted to stage a takeover, how could she and Robert possibly stop them? She and Robert should have given themselves up. She should have talked Robert out of ever starting in the first place. To be fair, what she should have done was go back to Anchorage with her

97

father. More than that, she should never have come up to Alaska to begin with. All the should-haves that now would never be.

At the reminder of her father, Annie was suddenly homesick. If the world was about to come apart at the seams, she wanted to be home when it happened. If only wishing could make it so, or clicking her magic red shoes together like Dorothy did to return home from Oz. Annie felt so far from home right now, she might as well be in Oz. She didn't even know she was crying until she saw a wet spot on her sweater. Quickly she dried her eyes and looked over at Robert to see if he had noticed, but in his concentration he hadn't moved a muscle.

Annie sighed. She was tired, terribly tired. She pulled Glenn's space blanket from his pack and wrapped up in it, using his pack for a pillow. She was asleep instantly.

"Okay, chow's on."

At the touch of a hand on her shoulder, Annie jerked awake. She had been dreaming, but right away, Robert's touch and the smell of food woke her up. She sat up and groaned. Her hands were still sore from paddling and she was tight all across her back and shoulders.

Robert smiled sympathetically as she tried to work out the stiffness. "You're just not used to using those muscles."

Another groan. "I guess not."

Annie must have been asleep a long time, long enough for Robert to have caught two char, cleaned and cooked them over a willow fire.

"Delicious," she said as she pulled the sweet oily meat apart with eager fingers, "and it's cooked perfectly."

"This makes up for the char we never got to eat for dinner last night." Robert finished the last of his fish, tossed the remains in the river, threw water over the rocks where he had been eating, then carefully washed his hands and face in the river.

98

"Rinse everything good and if you spilled any fish on you, wash it out," Robert called back over his shoulder.

Why the fuss? Annie started to wipe her hands on her blue jeans, then remembered, if a pine needle falls, a deer can hear it, an eagle can see it and a bear can smell it. That was why Robert was being so careful. Don't leave any trace of fish on you for a bear to smell. Annie hurriedly washed off her mouth and face and scrubbed her hands in the frigid water until they were red and smarting.

Although there was no sign yet of night, the sun was slowly slipping lower, the river seemed darker and the air was perceptibly cooler. Annie zipped up her parka, took Glenn's wool cap from his pack and pulled it down over her ears.

"You look a lot better in that than Glenn docs." Robert put his arm around Annie's shoulders in a familiar way and gave her a hug. Remembering the look that had passed between them in the mud tub, and the kiss they had exchanged back on the riverbank, Annie sensed a soft warmth spread through her. She remembered, too, Robert's strong arms, covered now by his shirt, and his muscular body pressed against hers when they were fishing yesterday.

"I think I look even better in Glenn's cap than you do in yours." Annie teasingly pulled Robert's baseball cap down over his eyes, surprised at her own boldness.

"But this is my lucky cap and nothing beats that." Robert pushed it back up with the tip of his forefinger. "You're okay, Short. And you're nice and quiet. I like that."

"In a family of talkers, I'm the only listener."

"Talk doesn't mean anything. It's what you do that counts and you're gutsy."

Annie had to laugh. "No one ever called me gutsy before." Although she minimized the compliment, she was startled . . . and pleased.

Robert cupped her small face in his hands. "And you've got

the nicest eyes I've ever seen. They change color from gray to green to blue." His voice caressed her.

Annie saw the sun directly over Robert's shoulder, not yet set, but definitely lower. The day wouldn't last forever, and if they wanted to stay warm tonight, they'd have to sleep close together by the fire. All of a sudden, Annie had the feeling that she was getting in over her head. She smiled tentatively and took a step backwards.

"I'm a chameleon and change moods like my eyes. One minute I'm hot and the next minute I'm cold, and right now, I guess I'm cold."

Robert looked at her a moment, dropped his hands from her shoulders, then kissed her on the forehead. "Okay, chameleon, if that's the way you want it, I'll go along."

The kiss was like a pledge that for the time being, any making out was on hold. Annie felt both a sense of regret and relief, regret because she realized she really liked and respected Robert, and relief because she didn't know what lay ahead in the next few days and her circuits were overloaded enough without adding any more input.

Robert didn't seem offended. Without further comment, he cleaned up the campsite, kicked at the fire, scattered the hot embers, and shouldered Norman's backpack.

"What are you doing?"

"It's time to push off."

That couldn't be. It would be night before long. "I . . . I thought we'd spend the night here by the fire." The fire was warmth and safety and protection.

"We're not going to spend the night anywhere. You had a long nap so we'll walk all night and keep going until we hit Niyuk. We oughtta be there by late tomorrow, or maybe the following day."

Annie stared. That would mean two nights in the tundra, exposed to the Russians . . . exposed to the bears . . .

100

Robert saw Annie's expression and tried to ease the blow with a smile. "We've got at least fifteen miles to go and we can't make more'n a mile an hour at best. We're not exactly walking on Astroturf, you know."

Yes, Annie did know and no, the smile didn't help. It had never occurred to her that they wouldn't spend the night here by the river, then reach Niyuk the next day.

There was obviously not going to be any discussion. Robert led the way through the brush and out on the other side. Although a rolling slope behind the brush had cut off any view of the land beyond, now, in the flat dusky light, the full panorama of the tundra lay before them, dappled here and there with scraps of fall colors and broken by familiar gray talus slopes. After the crackling little fire on the sheltered river-bank, Annie needed time to marshal her forces and orient herself to the vastness of the country and the blast of damp wind that blew in from the west. Apparently Robert had no such reservations. He just strode ahead, setting one foot resolutely in front of the other and Annie, with no other alternative, hurried after him.

18

Although the terrain was bumpy and full of uneven tussocks that gave way underfoot, at least the tundra was drier here than where Annie and Robert had surveyed earlier. And Robert was good at finding game trails that started abruptly in the middle of nowhere and ended just as abruptly in the middle of nowhere. Maybe we'll find one long game trail from here to Niyuk, Annie fantasized as she followed Robert through a particularly hillocky stretch.

Despite her nap back by the river, Annie was still stiff and she had a hard time keeping up with Robert's long strides. At first she tried stepping in his footprints, but because there was no way she could maintain that pace, she had to settle for taking two steps for every one of his. It was hard work, especially since she felt compelled to check constantly to her rear for something with four feet, as well as in the air overhead for something with a motor.

The sky was aflame now. Brilliant salmon pinks and crimsons were slapdashed in enormous strokes, with the sun a blinding sphere of blood-red. An old rhyme from childhood ran through Annie's head. "Red sky at night, sailors' delight.

102

Red sky in the morning, sailors take warning." Good. Violent and spectacular as the sunset was, it predicted good weather for tomorrow.

Aflame or not the sun radiated no heat, and the cold was beginning to penetrate through long underwear, jeans, parka and everything else. Annie's hands were numbly cold too, but at least the wind was dying down and Glenn's wool cap kept her ears warm. There was no question about it, she was running out of steam, and now, with the sun setting, it became increasingly hard to see. Annie found herself stumbling and tripping in the half-light as she struggled to keep up.

"Robert," she called, her clouded breath coming in quick puffs.

When Robert turned around, there was her face, framed by Glenn's rough wool cap, looking small and pinched and miserable.

"You about ready for a pit stop, Short?"

They were in a patch of dry open land that was overgrown with a mattress of springy ground cover.

"Yes." Wheezing, Annie inelegantly wiped her nose with her sleeve.

Robert eased off his backpack and helped Annie out of hers. "We can rest here where it's dry."

With every muscle in her body tight and sore, Annie sank down on her pack and closed her eyes, not realizing that Robert had kneeled in front of her until she felt his hands on her leg. He rubbed and massaged first one leg and then the other, kneading the calves especially.

"Relax," he ordered.

Considering the circumstances, that was easier said than done. "Do you think the Russians are following us, Robert?" Annie shivered at the memory of those bullets.

When Robert didn't answer, Annie persisted. "Do you think the Russians are following us or not?"

103

Robert kept on rubbing and kneading without looking up. "Maybe. Like I said, they must know where we're headed and they have a lot to lose if they don't stop us."

There, they *were* in danger. Annie had insisted on an answer, and now that she had it, she wished she had never asked.

Robert moved around behind Annie and started massaging her back and shoulders. He pounded and thumped in the most renewing way. "Hey, Short, if you want a little perspective, take a look at the sky. How's that for a sight?"

Annie looked up. She hadn't realized that day had made its final transition into night. Now she saw a star. And another. The sky was sprinkled with an infinity of stars. Annie had never seen anything like it. "Why . . . why, it's beautiful," she acknowledged.

Robert took off Annie's cap and began to massage her neck and the back of her head all the way up into her curly, hopelessly tangled hair.

"Look north and you'll see the Great Bear constellation, Ursa Major. This far above the Arctic Circle, it's almost directly overhead. See, the stars in the Big Dipper are the back part of the bear."

Annie squinted at the star-filled sky. With nothing to impede her view, the Milky Way was a wide pathway of light across the whole heavens, and yes, she could make out the Big Dipper.

"Now follow the line of the two stars in the bowl of the Big Dipper and you'll see our guiding north star, the polestar."

There it was, bright, dominant, stationary.

"The nine stars of the Big Dipper and the polestar on a field of blue is the Alaskan state flag."

It seemed appropriate somehow, and the longer Annie looked, the more stars there seemed to be, so that it was almost impossible to take in the sky's totality. Annie knew that Robert was only trying to distract her, but for the first time, she had

104

some kind of understanding of what this land and its limitless skies were all about for those, like Robert, who loved it.

After a good rest, Annie and Robert started out again. Fortunately there wasn't much night activity, just a series of whistles that Robert said was an owl, the rustling of little creatures in the brush, the murmur of a nearby stream. Once Annie saw the wobbly shadow of a porcupine and kept her distance. Although she was startled by the lumpish mounds scattered here and there on the tundra, Robert reassured her that they were only sleeping caribou.

The moon's luminous light, though not as intense as the sun, was bright enough to see by. And with that familiar strip of light on the horizon, total darkness didn't last much more than an hour. Soon the whole sky began to lighten, not with the drama of last night's sunset, but with the soft luster of a new morning. At the first sign of dawn, the birds started up their usual racket and the caribou heaved themselves to their feet with that peculiar clicking noise they made with each step. Annie took a careful look around. At least nobody was following them that she could see, and no hump-shouldered animal, fat and deceptively lazy-looking, was sauntering across the tundra.

The sun grew warm. Annie, who had already taken off her parka, now pulled off her sweater too. A line of moisture dotted her forehead, though that was more from the effort of trying to keep up with Robert than from the heat. And her pack was so heavy, she was bent over with its weight.

"This pack weighs a ton. Can I get rid of Glenn's rain stuff?"

"No, the weather's too unpredictable, but give them to me and I'll carry them for you."

Although the early morning sky was the same azure blue as yesterday's, with only a few puff clouds on the horizon, Annie didn't argue as she handed over the rain gear. That was a help, especially since the ground was wetter here and harder to walk on. The back of Annie's heel where her boot rubbed was beginning to bubble into a blister and the stream up ahead, where Robert had said they would stop for a drink, seemed just as far away now as it had half an hour ago.

And then between one step and the next, Annie could hardly move. She was totally exhausted, with every muscle in her body protesting. The stream, she only had to make it to the stream, but by the time she finally staggered up to it, all she could do was collapse on the ground beside Robert without even the strength to scoop up the water and drink. She lay still for a few minutes before making the effort to get the water from the river to her mouth. To her surprise, it tasted wonderful; she hadn't realized how thirsty she was.

She drank the freezing water until her teeth hurt, but when she turned to speak to Robert, he had gotten up, forded the shallow stream and was walking south away from her. If he expected her to follow, he could forget it. She wasn't going to budge. With a last regretful glance at Robert's retreating back, Annie wiped the water from her mouth, curled up on the sun-warmed rocks and closed her eyes.

"Wake up. I brought you some berries."

Half-asleep, Annie looked up at Robert. The sun was shining right in her eyes so it was hard to see, but something was wrong with him. His mouth and teeth and chin were purple. Still dazed, she glanced down at his cupped hands thrust in front of her. They were filled with blueberries and stained the same purple color.

"Come on, sit up and eat," he ordered, holding the berries up to her mouth.

Annie automatically started chewing and the sweet juice ran down her throat.

"There's a blueberry patch on the other side of the stream, so get off your butt and let's go."

Annie was too tired. "I can't, Robert. You go ahead." She closed her eyes.

106

"Stay here then, I'm not going to carry you." With that, Robert picked up Annie's backpack and strode on ahead about a hundred feet where he stopped and began to pick blueberries.

Blueberries. The taste of them was rich in Annie's mouth. She pushed herself up to a sitting position, then stood. Carry her? Who said anything about being carried? She'd make it to the blueberry patch on her own. And she did. Robert turned when he saw her and grinned, showing a straight, perfect line of purple teeth.

Annoyed as she was with him, Annie laughed.

"You don't look so good yourself, Short." Robert's face reflected the relief he felt. She was on her feet and moving, even laughing. He pointed to a low limestone eruption that was more a series of ledges than a mountain. "We'll stop at that talus slope. It'll make a good lookout to see if we're being followed, and we'll rest a while. We've earned it."

For the first time, Annie noticed circles under Robert's eyes and fatigue lines pinching his mouth. He was tired too. "How much longer . . ."

"Listen, do you hear that?" Robert looked up, scanning the sky.

Annie didn't hear anything. "What?"

"A motor . . . a plane . . ."

Annie's head snapped up. Now she heard the motor too. The Russians had come for them. They had been found out. But there was no place to hide, no trees, no brush, nothing. It was over.

"What can we do?"

"Quiet, I want to hear what direction it's coming from." Robert paused. "It's out of the southeast, probably from Kotz. That means it's not Soviet aircraft. I gotta signal them." Robert grabbed his pack off the ground and unbuckled it with frantic fingers. He snatched out his space blanket and started running.

Annie stood poised with a handful of berries halfway to her mouth. Dad! Why hadn't she thought of that before? It was Dad coming back. Everything would be okay. Dad would take over. Dad would know what to do. A sob of relief choked in Annie's throat.

Robert had already reached the bottom of the talus slope and was scrambling up its steep sides. Hurry, Annie urged him on as she realized what he was going to do, signal the plane with his space blanket. Sunlight was sure to flash off its reflective side, making Robert visible for miles. Annie clenched her fists so tight, her nails dug into her palms. Hurry, hurry, so Dad will see you.

At last she saw the plane too. It was flying south of them headed for the coast, although she still couldn't see what color it was. It just had to be a red-and-white Cessna.

Robert was almost to the top, finding a foothold here, a handhold there, stopping every once in a while to wave his blanket just in case he could be seen. He was only ten feet or so from the top when it happened. His foot slipped, loosening a rock that bounded and tumbled all the way to the bottom. That rock loosened another, and then another. Desperately, Robert grabbed for a more secure handhold, but it was too late. A whole section of ledge gave way under him and with a yell of surprise and a flash of the silver blanket, Robert fell in a clatter of bouncing stones and pebbles.

19

Above the sound of the motor, Annie heard the wind whining across the open tundra and the chirping squeal of a sik-sik. It was the almost human cry of the sik-sik that galvanized Annie, and she started running toward the talus slope fifty yards or so away. Robert lay curled up in a tight ball halfway down the slope where an outcropping had broken his fall. But he didn't move or call out or give any indication that he was even alive.

"Robert! Robert!" Annie shrieked as she slopped through a soggy stretch and scooted around the wobbly tussocks. Move. Get up. Say you're fine, she willed. But Robert just lay there, motionless.

As Annie started up the talus slope toward him, she noticed the plane. It was close enough now for her to see it was a small blue Super Cub and not Dad in the company Cessna after all. Her disappointment was so keen she could taste the bile of it in her mouth.

"Help! We need help!" She waved her arms and yelled. But they didn't see or hear her, and the little plane kept on its straight course toward the coast.

It couldn't just leave them here. "Help! Help!"

People, first aid, a radio, rescue. The receding plane had everything on board that she and Robert needed. The sound of its motor persisted long after it was just a speck in the Arctic sky. But Annie had no time to waste on regrets. She had to get to Robert. As she climbed the last twenty feet over the lichen-covered rocks, little stones loosened under her feet and tumbled down the slope. Careful, she had to be careful. She couldn't risk a fall too.

She dreaded reaching Robert. What if he was . . . was . . . She couldn't even form the words. Then, as she leaned over him, she saw his chest going in and out and she closed her eyes with a quick prayer of thanks.

"Robert, can you hear me?"

He was curved into a tight fetal position with his fists clenched. His baseball cap was gone and a cut on his forehead oozed blood.

"Don't touch me," he whispered as tears seeped out from under his squeezed-tight eyelids.

Annie literally wrung her hands with helplessness. She had to do something. Anything. Get the blanket. Cover him up. By the time she had retrieved the space blanket from where it had fallen and tucked it around him, his body had begun to relax a little. He even turned and looked up at her as she bent over him, and although his eyes were dull, he seemed to recognize her.

"Wind knocked out of me . . . give me a minute . . ." Again he closed his eyes, this time for so long, Annie wasn't sure if he was conscious or not.

She bit her lip and waited. At least they were out of the wind here and the sun was brightly warm. Trying not to panic, she forced herself to look out over the plains. That Russians might be following them was her first concern. No, she didn't see anything on the tundra that looked like people. Nor did she

110

see anything on the twisting Lanatak River that might be a mud tub or a raft. But the Lanatak was such a short distance back. Was that all the distance they had covered?

"Short . . ."

Annie spun around. Robert was on his back, propped up on his elbows. Although his face was still pale, at least it wasn't that awful putty gray it had been at first.

"Are you all right, Robert? What happened?" What a stupid question. He'd fallen, that's what happened.

"It's my ankle . . . I think I've broken it . . ." His chin was scraped raw and one eye was beginning to close.

What a relief. It was only his ankle, plus the wind had been knocked out of him. It wasn't as bad as she had first thought. "Do you want me to take your boot off?"

"No, the boot will keep the swelling down." Robert eased himself up to a sitting position, panting with the effort. "But get my gun and holster off me. My whole side hurts . . . I may have broken a rib . . ."

As Annie gingerly took the gun out of its holster, laid it on the ground and unfastened the holster strap, her mind began to mesh into gear. A broken ankle and maybe a broken rib. But that meant Robert couldn't walk.

"If my rib is broken, it could puncture a lung." Like a frightened child, Robert's eyes beseeched Annie to contradict him, and it stunned her to realize he was afraid. But he couldn't be. He was her strength, her rock, the only thing that kept her going.

"No, no, you won't puncture a lung. And probably your ankle is just sprained and not broken at all." Although her words ran all together in a not very convincing way, it was the best she could do. Robert was looking to her for reassurance and she had none to give.

Robert must have sensed her panic. "You're right. I'll be

111

okay. Just go get our packs, will you?" he asked and Annie tried not to notice the tears of pain and frustration in his eyes.

Picking up the packs took quite a while. Annie delivered Robert's first, then went back for hers. By the time she returned, huffing and panting, Robert had pulled himself into a protected recess and was propped up against the cliffside. Moss grew in scattered patches on the slope, but the ledge they were on was overgrown with leathery lichens. In an attempt to make him more comfortable, Annie tucked his backpack behind his head.

"If one plane went over, maybe there'll be others." Robert's voice was shaky.

Annie grabbed at the suggestion. "As soon as we hear a plane, I'll start waving the space blanket. They'll see us this time, won't they?"

Optimism turned out to be more than Robert could manage. "We're not exactly on the main airline route."

Annie wished he had never brought up the subject. Now she had to admit that in all the time she'd been at Little Salmon, she had never heard or seen a plane or helicopter other than their own. But what about Dad? He'd be flying back soon to pick her up.

"Dad will be back . . ." She counted on her fingers ". . . tomorrow, or is it the day after?" The long days and brief nights had her completely confused.

Robert didn't answer. He was asleep. Or unconscious. Either way, now that he was relaxed, Annie could see how badly bruised his face was. At least the cut on his forehead had stopped bleeding, though his eye was puffy and already beginning to discolor. She covered him with both space blankets and sat with her knees drawn up to her chest leaning against her backpack.

Right now everything depended on Dad. On his way to Little Salmon, she'd signal him from right here with the space blankets and he'd know what to do. She and Robert would just have to manage the best they could until then. Luckily there was the blueberry patch and a stream nearby for food and water, and Robert could tell her how to build a fire. They could hold out until Dad came. They would have to.

But Annie had to acknowledge the leaden weight in the pit of her stomach. It wasn't that simple. This little talus slope wasn't on Dad's route to camp. On their trip out to Little Salmon, Dad had flown out of his way to show her Niyuk, she remembered him telling her that, and this time he was sure to fly straight to camp. Camp. When Dad buzzed camp to let them know he had arrived and saw the burned-out helicopters, he'd be worried about her and anxious to land. And landing would put him in danger.

Robert groaned and his unfocused eyes flickered open. "Have to . . . get . . . there . . ." he mumbled.

Get to Niyuk was what Robert meant. He had been determined to reach Niyuk no matter what. Even now, injured and in pain, he was dreaming about it. A risk-taker was what Robert was. Those defectors had been risk-takers too, crossing the Chukchi Sea in a fishing boat in an attempt to prevent what could be a terrible catastrophe.

Annie closed her eyes to shut off her thoughts, but as soon as she did, she visualized mushroom clouds and firestorms and devastated cities, all possibilities again. And the figures were no longer impersonal statistics. Every name at Little Salmon had a face, Mac and Willy Lou and Lester and Val and Glenn and Beers and Norman. And now Dad would be caught up in it too. All the take-charge people who were no longer in charge.

That left one person. Her. Annie leaned her head back and looked up at the sky. The few low clouds on the horizon had swelled, but the sky above was as blue as ever. A bird soared so high overhead it was only a dot. Robert moaned again in his sleep, and when she looked at him, he was turning and twisting his head as if to get away from a nightmare.

She was utterly and completely alone. There was no one in the whole world to tell her what to do, and this time she couldn't back off into a no-decision decision. This time she had to come to grips with her choices—either stay here with Robert and hope that help would come, or try to make it to Niyuk on her own.

The strange part was that for someone who agonized over what to wear to school every morning, Annie didn't take long to make her decision. With Robert lying only a couple of feet away breathing a scary kind of rattly snore and moaning in his sleep, she knew she had to get help. Dad was involved too. If she didn't reach Niyuk in time to stop him, he would take off for Little Salmon. Besides, if she started right away, she would have a better chance of staying ahead of any Russians that might be following them. Yes, she decided, she'd do it, hike to Niyuk on her own.

Not that she wasn't terrified. As she opened Glenn's pack to check out the contents, tears welled up in her eyes. She brushed them angrily away. Tears weren't going to help now. Nevertheless, she couldn't keep her hands from shaking as she laid everything out, and she had better get Glenn's rain gear out of the other pack too. Although the sun was still out, heavy low clouds banked the horizon.

Carefully she slipped the pack out from under Robert's head, stuffing his parka in its place. Robert opened his eyes. "I'm not asleep," he murmured.

"It's okay. Take it easy," she assured him. Without even realizing it, Annie's tone of voice indicated that she, not Robert, was now in charge. She took out Glenn's rain jacket and overalls, folded them up and put them in her own backpack with the rest of the equipment.

Robert was watching her. "You're going to Niyuk." It wasn't a question.

114

Annie nodded.

"Listen to me . . ." Robert grimaced as he tried to shift into a more comfortable position. "Head due south by the compass . . . the sun will be south at noon so keep walking into the sun . . . at night any horizon light from the sun will be due north . . . call the Air Force base when you get to Niyuk. Stay away from bear caches . . . never run from a bear . . . anything running means game . . . freeze or curl up and play dead . . ."

No, Annie didn't want to hear this. If she listened and took it seriously, she might not have the courage to start.

Robert had only paused to catch his breath. "You'll see a mountain, it looks like a big church . . . it's called the Cathedral . . . Niyuk is just south of that." Robert tried to smile but his lip was so swollen it came out all lopsided. Annie had to give him credit. She couldn't muster up any kind of smile, straight *or* lopsided.

There was a lot to do before Annie could start out. Following Robert's instructions, she gathered as many twigs as she could find, built a fire and left everything he would need within his easy reach. He insisted that she take most of the leftover food from the packs, as well as one of the space blankets. Although Annie knew there was no way she was going to lie down out in the tundra and risk falling asleep, she took it, more to use as a signal flag than anything else.

"Here's my gun." Robert held out his gun to her, butt first.

Annie stared at it. The gun substantiated an unpleasant fact, the very real danger she would be facing. But that was too much to cope with and she shook her head. "No, I wouldn't know how to use it. Besides, you might need it." Neither of them mentioned the possibility of the Russians finding Robert . . . or the kind of helpless prey he made for animals lying here unprotected on the ledge.

He didn't argue. "Before you go, come here," he said. Suddenly Robert's familiar face looked very dear as he reached

115

up and put his arm around her. "You'll make it, Annie. Like I said, you're gutsy."

Annie leaned down and pressed her cheek against his and both their cheeks were wet and she didn't know if that was from her tears or his. There was no embrace, no kiss. But that lingering moment when their cheeks met, cool and wet, was more special than anything that had passed between them before. And the "Annie" helped. Robert was giving her an adult status that the "Short Straw" had denied her.

As Annie strapped on her backpack, Robert watched soberly. He was worried, she could tell, but she couldn't let it get to her or she might just give up the whole crazy idea. And then she was ready. She wished Robert a quick goodbye and started down the slope, concentrating on one step at a time. She was almost to the bottom when she noticed Robert's good luck baseball cap caught between two rocks. When she picked it up, she was instantly aware of its Robert-smell, a combination of warmth, perspiration and dirt. She put it on and turned to check if Robert had seen her. He was still lying next to the fire where she had left him, but he waved gamely with a half-raised arm.

"So long, Annie. Give it to 'em."

His thin voice threaded down to her. That was it. The last voice she would hear for a long time. Alone, she was all alone. Not alone in the house at night with everyone gone and the old floorboards creaking. Not alone walking back from Lisa's in the dark with only the street lamps to light her way. This was alone in the widest, most complete sense it was possible to experience.

20

Robert had found Annie a long stick from his pile of twigs for her to use as a walking staff and now she swung out with it, away from the talus slope. South, she had to keep heading south. Straight ahead, the sun shone in her eyes, but just to make sure she was going in the right direction, she pulled her compass from her blue jeans' pocket and held it steady the way Robert had showed her. The red needle pointed behind her to North. Good, at least the compass worked and she knew how to use it.

For the first time, Annie looked ahead. Ahead was miles and miles of open ground, broken on both the east and west by low talus slope mountains. Although being out in the field those few days with Robert had acclimated her somewhat, Annie still had no sense of distance, and the mountains could have been anywhere from five to twenty miles away. One fact she was sure of, there were more barren ground caribou migrating than she had ever seen before. They were moving slowly in groups of ten or fifteen, most of them headed south like she was, so that all she saw was their white rumps and arched antlers jutting up over their backs as they grazed.

117

Although the caribou gave no indication they were aware of her, they kept their distance, eighty or ninety yards away, but even so, Annie could smell their rank odor and hear that strange click-click they made as they moved. She found their presence enormously comforting; she couldn't imagine the caribou migrating at such a leisurely pace or grazing so serenely if there were bears anywhere around. Nevertheless, she kept a sharp eye out in all directions for anything large with a rolling gait and a distinguishing hump. At least for the time being, she felt a little less paranoid about the Russians. From their vantage point on the ledge, neither she nor Robert had been able to see evidence of anyone following them.

Besides, for the moment, Annie was having other problems. She soon learned that the greener and lusher the tundra looked, the wetter it was underfoot. As she headed across what looked like a lovely green meadow, she found herself slogging through what was almost a marsh, patchy with miserable tussocks. And the terrain surrounding the tussocks was a mat of thick low growth and twisted ground cover that tripped her up. Because the land was so flat, the water couldn't run off, and with soil that was only a couple of feet deep before becoming permafrost, the ground couldn't absorb it either. So there it sat, slowing her down to practically a crawl.

Annie tramped through the wretched quagmire for what seemed like hours. Her right foot rubbed her heel, the calves of her legs were in tight knots, and her back and shoulders ached under the burden of her pack. But when she turned around, the talus slope where she'd left Robert was still in view behind her, appearing almost as large as when she'd first started out. She wasn't even making a mile an hour.

Food and water would help. She'd passed through a couple of berry patches without stopping. The bright red berries were probably edible, but she didn't know what they were and was afraid to try them. Then up ahead she saw a stream. At least she saw a break in the tundra with a line of low willows and alder that she had learned meant running water. She'd make that stream her target, and when she reached it, she'd stop and drink and eat the Hershey bar Robert had insisted she bring with her. The stream became her goal and she wouldn't let herself think beyond it.

But the longer Annie walked, the farther away the line of willows seemed to get. Maybe they were a mirage, like seeing a lake in the middle of a desert. Then two ducks landed on the other side of the brush and Annie knew it wasn't a mirage. Where there were ducks, there had to be water.

As Annie continued toward the stream she realized she was hurrying through a blueberry patch. At the sight of the fat shiny berries, all the hunger juices in her stomach began to churn and she could feel her mouth start to water. She ate a couple of handfuls, then unstrapped her backpack and took out her space blanket. Holding all four corners together to make a sling, she began to fill the blanket. But as Annie finished with one bush and moved to another, she spotted bear scat not five feet away. Although she had never seen bear scat before, there was no mistaking it. It wasn't steaming, but it was bluish and full of hairs as if the bear had eaten some animal whole.

Annie staggered back, grabbed her pack from off the ground and ran out of the blueberry patch as fast as she could, spilling blueberries the whole way. Her heartbeat filled her entire chest so that it was hard to breathe.

The scat is old. Don't panic. Stop. Look and make sure no bears are around. Annie forced herself to do all those things. Little voles scurried underfoot, birds were settling down for the night, the grazing caribou still seemed unconcerned. It was okay. That bear must have been here days ago, maybe weeks. Although all Annie wanted now was to reach that stream, she couldn't seem to get her heartbeat started up in a regular way

119

again, and she puffed and panted as she struggled through the spongy tundra, still holding on to what was left of her berries.

She was almost there, only about fifty feet away, when two wide branches on the far bank emerged out of the low willows. Only they weren't branches, they were wide antlers and under the antlers was a long, morose face. A moose.

The moose must have been lying down. Now, with some kind of green plant hanging from its right antler, it rose to its full height. If the animal hadn't been so frighteningly enormous, he would have looked ridiculous, but he was beyond any size that Annie had ever imagined an animal could be. He must have been seven feet high at the shoulder, with five-foot-wide antlers. As he swung his head with its great drooping nose in her direction, his small eyes blinked and his ears twitched.

Annie couldn't think of anything, not running away, or shouting or fainting. She was completely mesmerized as the moose stared at her and she stared at him. Wait, was this the mating season? Dad had said that a moose in rut during mating season or a cow with calves was dangerous. But this moose didn't seem dangerous. The absurd word that came to Annie's mind was "interested." Robert had said that caribou and moose led boring lives and anything out of the ordinary interested them. But what if he was so interested he crossed the stream and came over to investigate her?

Annie, who had momentarily stopped breathing, took a quick gulp of air. Now the adrenaline was going full force as she carefully put one foot behind her, then another. The ground was so uneven, she had to grope around to find a solid footing. One step, another step, all the time keeping her eyes on the moose.

But with the next step, she caught her foot in a twisted root and lost her balance. With a yelp of surprise, she fought to stay on her feet, but it was too late, and she fell, landing on her back with the air knocked out of her. Like an overturned turtle, she fought to right herself as she choked back a scream.

120

The moose took a tentative step backward, then stopped, lowered his head, then turned and walked away, the ludicrous green plant still dangling from his antler. With each step, his big hooves sucked at the muck.

Annie rolled over onto her hands and knees and watched the moose trot away in an awkward sort of gait. Despite his homely face, sway back and short body set on long spindly legs, dignified was how Annie would have described him. Dignified and beautiful, in his own way.

As Annie followed the moose's retreat across the tundra, a rush of self-knowledge flowed through her. She had faced down a moose without totally panicking. This was his world, not hers, and for a moment she had been a part of it. Correction, he had *allowed* her to be a part of it, and she had come through it intact with no one telling her how to handle the situation. Not Dad. Not Robert.

Annie looked around at the caribou slowly migrating south on the same route herds had taken for centuries. She glanced at the moose, not much more than a dark silhouette now in the early evening light, the ducks calmly swimming in the stream, the sik-siks that were like old chattery friends. In that moment, the tundra didn't seem so desolate, nor did Annie feel so completely alone. In a new and satisfying way, she no longer felt like a stranger in a foreign land.

21

Annie drank deeply from the stream. In its purity, the water glimmered apple green as it splashed over the same rocks it had splashed over for years, maybe centuries. She was probably the first person to drink from this stream, and at that moment, alone took on a new meaning. Alone meant being the only one, the first. It was the solitude that Robert had talked about. Solitude and alone, Annie realized, were two different conditions.

Poking into the water with her staff to make sure it wasn't over her boots, Annie forded the stream and sat down to rest on the far bank, not far from where she had first seen the moose. She laid out her space blanket with its remaining few berries and opened her backpack. The sun was so flat it was only a sliver of red in a dark and lowering sky with no promise of a brilliant sunset to delight a sailor. But as Annie ate her berries, she wouldn't let herself think ahead to morning.

Right now she had to think about tonight and how to get through it. Darkness was closing in and there would be no moon to light her way or polestar to guide her. She would have to find a place to stop until morning. Robert had told her to pick the highest, driest spot, out of the wind. And she needed dryness. She was wet through where she had fallen, and she could already feel a damp chill seep through her. She needed to take off her boots too, and see to her blistered heel.

Although there weren't many twigs, she gathered up as many as she could find, and as she did, she thought about Robert and wondered if his fire was holding out. Maybe a fire up on that ledge hadn't been such a good idea. If any Russians had been following, the fire would lead them right to Robert . . . on the other hand, a fire would keep any animals away. But she couldn't spend time worrying about Robert. Right now she had to get going. The low rolling mountain up ahead would be her destination.

Having a plan of action gave Annie a sense of confidence that was new to her, although the mountain, like everything else on the tundra, seemed to retreat the farther she walked. By the end of an hour, her euphoria had evaporated into a state of leaden exhaustion, and it was getting dark more quickly than she had counted on.

Life had already stilled down for the night. The birds had long since ceased any activity and the caribou seemed sluggish and drowsy, with some of them just standing around while others had already laid down. Sluggish and drowsy was fine with Annie. Sluggish and drowsy meant there was no immediate threat of bears.

"Hay foot, straw foot," Annie suddenly muttered under her breath, startling even herself. Probably it was because she had a walking staff in one hand and a bundle of twigs in the other that she was reminded of the year in gym when they had marched in formation, calling out "hay foot, straw foot" with each step. Ms. Carson had told them that during the Revolutionary War, if a soldier didn't know his left foot from his right, he held a piece of hay in one hand and straw in the other and marched to the cadence of "hay foot, straw foot."

The "straw foot" made Annie think of Robert's Short Straw, and the way he had said she was gutsy. If he could see her now, he wouldn't call her that. Only her walking staff and the ridiculous "hay foot, straw foot" kept her going.

By the time Annie hobbled up to the talus slope, the light was so dusky she couldn't see her watch. But she knew it was late, probably close to midnight. With no moon or stars out, she had to tap her way up the incline with her walking staff like a blind person. A rustle over to the side, followed by a quick pattering, stopped Annie in her tracks as a small animal scurried out of her way. It was only a sik-sik. But she had to pause and catch her breath before she could go on. If only she had a flashlight, something to light her way, but all she had was matches, precious matches that she needed to start a fire.

About twenty feet up the slope, Annie found a bed of dry moss that was soft and springy and there was just enough light on the horizon for her to make out that she was safe here and not sharing the ledge with some furry or sharp-quilled creature.

By the time Annie finally got a sputtering fire started with her little pile of twigs and rolled-up toilet paper, she was so tense the top of her head was ready to blow off. It didn't seem possible that a simple fire could be so difficult to get going. And she was still cold. She laid out her space blanket, put on Glenn's extra shirt, and then pulled his wool hat down over Robert's baseball cap. Now for her feet. Off with the boots and socks. There was the blister, red and sore-looking, with a puffy white center. Annie stretched out her feet toward the feeble fire and wiggled her stiff toes. Although what she needed for the blister was a Band-Aid, she'd have to make do with what she had. Annie folded up a strip of toilet paper and laid it over the blister, pulled on her white sock liner and over that her wool sock. At least her rubber boots had kept her feet warm as well as dry.

124

Exhausted as she was, there was no question of sleeping. Every once in a while there was a sound from out on the tundra, a moan, the creaking of a restless caribou, weird, booming *whoo-whoos* that frightened her even though she knew it was only an owl. And she couldn't let her fire go out. She had to keep adding twigs, one by one. It was all that stood between her and whatever was out there, roaming, prowling, searching.

Think of something . . . anything . . . to stay awake. Go through your room at home, starting with the pink wallpaper that Dad had been promising to redo for years, on to the beautiful handmade quilt that Mom had found at an auction, the soft little shag rug by her bed that was the first thing her feet touched in the morning . . .

Now Annie was so cold she was trembling. She glanced dully at the fire, a smoldering, snaky ribbon of smoke that she had to keep going. Although the night was Arctic-short, it seemed endless as Annie used all her twigs for the fire, one by one, finally feeding even her walking stick to the feeble flames.

When dawn came, it was as gray and dreary as her pile of cold ashes. 3:02 read Annie's watch. But she felt so disoriented, she wasn't certain if that was A.M. or P.M. Cold was all she could think about and she knew if she didn't get going, she never would. She had to force herself to move, to pack up her belongings, ease her blistered foot into the boot, eat a couple of Life Savers and finish the rock-hard bologna sandwich Robert had persuaded her to take. Her throat was so sore this morning she could hardly swallow and her head ached. That was partly from hunger, she knew, but sometimes she got a dull headache like this before it rained. She gritted her teeth against the possibility. Please, no rain.

But she couldn't fool herself any longer. The dampness she felt on her face was rain and not just mist. It was coming out of the northwest, from the sea, and it had the smell of the sea

125

about it, dank and raw. Maybe she should stay here until the rain passed. The little mossy ledge had an overhang that would keep her relatively dry. She could find some blueberries to eat on the tundra and a day's rest would help both her blistered heel and her sore throat. Why not?

Annie knew why not. There was Robert, alone and hurt, counting on her. Everyone else was counting on her too. Even if she reached Niyuk too late to do anything about that Soviet missile base, even if something happened that she didn't make it at all, she knew she had to try. It was as simple, and complicated, as that.

As Annie worked her arms into her backpack and tied the straps around her waist to take the strain off her shoulders, she checked her compass. South. There it was. If only that mountain in the distance was the Cathedral, but there was no way she could fool herself into believing that it was anything more than another smooth rounded talus slope.

Now the mist had changed into something between rain and snow, a clammy drizzle that clung wetly to Annie's face and hair as she turned south. Her throat was raw and she missed the support of her walking staff. When the drizzle became large wet flakes of snow, for a while the going was easier, but as the snow began to accumulate, the whiteness hid the little depressions and hollows underfoot and the walking was almost impossible.

Annie had no idea how many hours she had been trudging along when she stumbled onto another blueberry patch. The blueberries were covered with snow, but the cold shock of them in her mouth helped revive her and the sweet juice soothed her throat. She had already started on her way again when she heard it. A motor. At first she thought maybe she was imagining it, but it was familiar and persistent, unquestionably an airplane motor.

The sound was louder now, but Annie couldn't see anything through the gray canopy of cloud cover, and what was worse, she couldn't tell what direction it was coming from. If it came from the west, it could be a Soviet plane searching for Robert and her. On the other hand, it could be that plane she and Robert had seen yesterday returning to Kotzebue from the coast. It could even be Dad, only she'd counted on that once before and been disappointed. All she could do was wait, low here in the blueberry bog, poised with her space blanket ready to signal. Still she could only hear the plane, not see it. Now the sound was fading, growing dimmer. But it couldn't be! The pilot had to see her and know that she was in trouble.

And then the sound of the motor disappeared and only the chatter of the morning birds and the creaking of the caribou broke the infinite silence. A couple of snowflakes caught in Annie's eyelashes, wreathing everything with a luminous halo that softened the tundra into a serene and beautiful landscape, beautiful enough just to lie down and give up. Annie was as tired as she was discouraged, and only visions of sleeping matchstick girls frozen in the snow prodded her on.

Reluctantly, she brushed herself off and headed south again. South. Annie conjured up images of south, palm trees and sandy beaches and the coconut smell of suntan lotion. South here just meant more snow. Snow in August. Or maybe it wasn't August anymore. She didn't know what day it was, so who was to say what month it was?

Annie sensed her mind going off on crazy tangents. Although she knew she had to keep her head on straight, her thoughts insisted on wandering . . . to Robert and if he was getting snow too . . . to the first time she had ever seen snow . . . to the ski weekend when she and Lisa had found a bottle of scotch and the two of them had gotten drunk instead of going skiing with everyone else . . . it was the only time she had ever been in trouble, until now . . . and now she was in the worst trouble of her life . . . if only she could stop and rest

127

. . . her throat hurt and the snow had turned to rain . . . everything would freeze . . .

Suddenly, out of her peripheral vision, Annie glimpsed an unhurried motion a good distance away, over to her left. Her first reaction was that she had been preoccupied by bears for so long, her imagination had invented it. But when she paused and took a good look, reality flooded through her. It *was* a bear. The animal's broad silvery back was flecked with snow as it padded along in the middle of a caribou herd with its large head swinging from side to side and its stride so effortless it seemed to be gliding. And there was that hump, that unmistakable hump. Incredibly, none of the caribou seemed to be in the least concerned.

Although it was a fair distance away, almost the length of two football fields, it was traveling southwest to Annie's due south. Terror-stricken as Annie was, she realized that if they both kept going their paths would cross.

Where was the bear in relation to her, upwind or downwind? Not that Annie knew which was the wrong way anyhow. All she knew was if the wind was coming from a certain direction, the bear would be able to smell her. And there was plenty to smell. She was radiating fear, sweat, panic, adrenaline, everything that the human body can produce in a crisis, including the blueberries she'd had for breakfast that hovered at the back of her throat ready to come up.

Run, that was her first thought. Bears have poor eyesight. It wouldn't see her, and she was certainly capable of running. Flying even.

A mental hand clapped down on her shoulder. Don't run. Anything running means game to a bear and a bear can outrun you any day. Don't move. It was an order. Annie stood stock still, her fists jammed in her pockets and her feet taking root, although not to move was almost more than she could tolerate. Every instinct demanded action, flee, scream, yell

128

her head off, anything to release the tension that had her close to hyperventilating.

All of a sudden there was a violent eruption of noise as twenty caribou or so took flight with a loud burst of grunts, clicking heel bones and clattering antlers. In a melee of white rumps and tails, the caribou spewed mud and snow in their headlong stampede. Something had spooked them as they sprinted a good distance, then stopped and milled around nervously.

Two shapes were still running. The bear had taken off after one of the caribou in an explosion of speed. Robert had said a caribou could outrun a bear any time unless it was too young or old or sick, and even from a distance, Annie could see that this caribou was limping. It headed for a shallow stream with the bear right on its tail. Taking a stand on a wide gravel bar, the caribou whirled to face its attacker with its head down and its huge antlers both a weapon and a shield. The bear was cautious, moving around those antlers, circling, backtracking, sizing up its prey. The bear probably weighed five hundred pounds, but it looked small next to the caribou, although far from helpless. It was a compact machine for killing, with every instinct and reflex geared to that goal.

The caribou, with its head still down, was backing away now, its hind legs already in the water. Without warning, the bear darted in and took a fast swipe at the caribou's neck. Simultaneously, the caribou thrust its antlers down and up, missing the bear only by inches. But in the moment it took the caribou to lower its antlers for another lunge, the bear moved in and raked its claws across the caribou's neck, bringing it down in a flurry of water and thrashing legs. The caribou struggled to get up, kicking its dangerous hooves and swinging its antlers toward the bear.

Both of them were in the water now as the bear ripped into the caribou with such ferocity the animal didn't have a chance. It gave a few futile kicks, then lay still. Now the bear clamped its teeth on the caribou's neck and dragged it out of the water up onto the gravel bar. The head, with its majestic rack of antlers, hung limp and broken as the bear stretched out full length and tore at its victim, turning the clear stream scarlet with blood.

At the sight of the blood, Annie realized she wasn't watching some wildlife special on TV, she was in the middle of it. She had to get out of here. Slowly, move slowly. Her rigid feet and legs moved backward so mechanically, it was as if she had been wound up by a key. She would have to circle well to the west to keep away from the bear, careful the whole time not to trip or fall in the slippery wet snow. Sore throat, blistered foot, fatigue, hunger, aching muscles, sleety rain, all were forgotten as Annie made her way stealthily, cautiously to safety.

22

Annie felt betrayed. She had been counting all along on those stupid caribou to warn her of danger, and here a bear had been right in the middle of their herd and until it had made its move, they hadn't even noticed it. Now, as she looked around, the widely scattered caribou began to blur, change shape, take on ominous forms. Annie told herself she was imagining things, that with a whole caribou for itself, the bear wasn't about to go anywhere, but fatigue and the cold had her groggy and confused.

The incident was unnerving in more ways than one. Though there had been no sign of any Russians following her, that didn't mean they had given up. They might have come by a different route, and could be hiding right now behind some talus slope waiting for her. It was possible they had already picked up Robert, taken him back to camp and were now on their way after her. Despite it all, bears, Russians, guns and rain, Annie realized there was nothing to do but keep going.

As she slogged through the muck, she tried to organize her thoughts into something concrete, like naming all fifty states, or listing the presidents, but she couldn't even muster up a "hay foot, straw foot." All she could cope with was the rain, the constant rain that beat down and turned everything to slush. Although Glenn's outsize rain gear was cumbersome and awkward, it did keep her relatively dry, except for her hair which straggled wetly across her face.

Even finding a blueberry patch didn't do much to lift Annie's spirits. She forced herself to eat the frozen berries because she knew they would relieve her throat and give her energy, but she was beyond hunger, and the cold berries not only hurt her teeth, but they also made her slightly sick to her stomach. More than that, she hated the feeling of being trapped in the low-lying hollow. At least this time she didn't see any bear scat, old or steaming.

Visibility was poor. Whether it was fog or low-lying clouds that had rolled in, Annie didn't know or care. All she knew was she couldn't see more than a hundred feet in front of her, let alone across the tundra to the mountains in the distance. As the afternoon progressed, Annie cared only about one thing, finding the Cathedral. The Russians, Little Salmon, Robert, Dad, it wasn't that they didn't matter anymore, it was just that she didn't have the strength to worry about anything beyond her own perimeters. Maybe the Cathedral was that mountain over there, the one with the deep crevice. But the rest of the mountain was rounded and smooth-looking, just another talus slope after all.

Annie readjusted her pack on her aching shoulders and scanned the horizon for the next mountain. But she didn't see any more, only a disjointed herd of caribou that looked as wet and dispirited as she felt. That was strange. They weren't going in the same direction she was. Although they didn't always travel in a direct line, they usually took a southerly course. Not this group. Unless . . . unless . . . it was she, and not the caribou, who was off course. With sudden clarity, Annie remembered she had made a wide westerly circle around that bear and had never gotten back on track again.

Annie pulled out her compass and held it steady, hardly daring to breathe as she lowered her eyes to look at it. Although north should have been directly behind her, it was off at a distinct angle. Annie felt no panic or fear, nothing but an overwhelming sense of hopelessness as everything crumbled, her determination, the last of her energy, any momentum she'd been able to maintain. She took off her backpack, dropped it on the ground and sank down on it.

Prayer. The word came to her, unbidden, but at that moment, she knew that was all she had left. Neither Annie nor her family were religious. Her parents had left the decision whether or not to go to church up to the three children, and after a year of Sunday School, Annie had never gone back. Consequently, it didn't seem right to pray now, like she had ignored God all these years and now when she was in trouble, she was asking for help. On the other hand, Annie realized that God was all she had going for her and if He chose to ignore her, that was up to Him.

That left a basic problem. She didn't know how to pray. She felt strangely embarrassed as she folded her hands and bowed her head the way she had learned in Sunday School.

"I'm not even sure You're there, but if You are, I need help," she said softly. "I'm lost and I don't think I can go on. Help me find the way." It sounded awfully demanding, Annie decided, so she added, "It's not just for me. It's for Robert and Dad and everyone at Little Salmon and . . . and for everyone else too . . ."

Whether it was the prayer or the short rest that got her going again, Annie never knew. She certainly didn't hear a clap of thunder or see a bolt of lightning through the gray downpour. All she heard was the steady slap of rain on her jacket and the distant quarreling of two ravens. The exhaustion and hunger and sore throat and blister and pain were all still there, but she realized that if she expected God to help, she was the one who would have to put one foot in front of the other. She stood up, shouldered her pack and started off, this time in a south-easterly direction.

Good resolutions or not, by the time Annie spotted the tell-tale willows and alders up ahead that indicated a stream, she was weaving and staggering like a drunk, and she felt like a drunk, too, woozy, lightheaded, uncoordinated. But she was alert enough to keep the creek as her goal. She pushed through four-foot-high willows, wary for anything that might be hiding behind them. When she finally reached the creek, its width caught her by surprise. It was a river, really, swift and wide where the snow and rain had swollen its banks. White water bubbled and coursed around smooth boulders on its rush from the mountains to the sea.

Annie foraged cautiously in the thicket until she found a long stick. It wasn't as sturdy as her old walking staff, but it would do for a measuring rod. But when she poked the stick into the river, it went down a good three feet. Whew, it was lucky she hadn't trusted her eyesight and tried to ford the river here. The rocks on the bottom were so clearly delineated, the water had looked safely shallow. She walked farther upstream, testing with her stick the whole way, but it was deep every-where.

At last she found it, a wide bend in the river where the water was slower and shallower, and where her stick went down only a foot and a half. She would have to count on it being shallow all the way across. She slipped out of Glenn's clumsy rain jacket and pants and stuffed them in her pack. But the water would be over her boots here. Hesitating only a moment, Annie rolled up her blue jeans, then took off her socks and boots and put them in her pack too. But now the pack was terribly heavy. Annie studied the width of the river, fifteen, maybe twenty feet across. Taking careful aim, she wound up and heaved the pack across the river to the other side. Plunk, it splashed in the water where it lay for a moment near the far

134

bank. Then as Annie watched helplessly, the current picked it up, swung it in circles and carried it away downstream.

Stupid! Stupid! She had never been any good at throwing, whatever made her think she could reach the other side? Annie clenched her fists in frustration and glared down at her bare feet. They looked white and ugly against the cold gray rocks. Get going. The only way you're going to make it to the other side is by plunging in.

Bracing herself on her staff, Annie gingerly put one foot in the water, and then the other. Instantly they went numb. Another step. Another. But the stream was swifter than she had anticipated and the current sucked and tugged at her. With all sensation gone, she could only feel a heavy pressure where her legs and feet should be. Annie took another step, but the stones on the bottom were rounded and slippery. Her numbed feet couldn't find a sure footing, and she was thrown off balance, tumbling backwards into the water.

Gasping from the frigid shock, Annie flailed out with her arms and struggled to regain her balance as the current bumped her over the rocks. She grasped the bottom with frozen fingers trying to get a grip, but she was swept a good ten feet downstream before she was able to stop her headlong flight. There, at last she steadied herself, instinctively pushing off toward shore. It was shallower here, but her legs were so leaden, it took her long moments to slide and stumble her way out of the water.

Coughing and wheezing, Annie lay on the rocky bank with water streaming off her and all feeling anesthetized out of her. She was finished. Her pack with everything in it was gone. She was soaking wet. Her clothes and hair would freeze. There was nothing left.

Vaguely, dimly, Annie heard trumpeting nearby, almost like a deep musical instrument, and she looked up. A pair of swans, huge and gloriously white, were flying by, their seven-

135

foot-wide wings in rhythm with each other as they called back and forth. It never occurred to Annie that they weren't calling to her as she followed their line of flight.

And there it was, right beyond the swans, a mountain crowned with spires and towers and steeples. It was unmistakably a cathedral, a medieval cathedral, waiting to take her in, and she was the pilgrim seeking its shelter.

23

Annie sat behind the pilot and the copilot in the big U.S. Coast Guard helicopter searching the tundra for Robert. Both pilots wore neatly pressed uniforms with no mirror reflecting glasses or bulging tobacco-stuffed cheeks. Although the paramedics had wanted Annie to ride in the back of the chopper on a stretcher, despite her burning throat and groggy sense of unreality, she had refused. She couldn't let down until they found Robert. If only she could remember exactly where she had left him, what the talus slope had looked like, how far it was from the Lanatak River. But the terrain below them was an endless confusion of similar-looking terrain, braided creeks and streams and identical limestone mountains.

Annie's own ordeal was over. She had reached Niyuk, something she hadn't ever been sure in her heart she could do. And maybe she hadn't really done it on her own. When everything was at its most hopeless, she had said a prayer that she'd make it to Niyuk, and she had. Although there was no way she could call that a simple coincidence, it was something she would file away to consider later, in private, when her thinking wasn't so fuzzy.

Actually Annie hadn't found Niyuk, Niyuk had found her. When she had finally staggered up to the Cathedral, four natives fishing in the Niyuk River had spotted her and come running to help. They had rushed her back to one of their fishing shacks where the women had dressed her in dry clothes, wrapped her in blankets and given her some kind of hot bitter tea. As Annie haltingly tried to explain what had happened, the little room had been crowded with concerned faces. Immediately, someone had phoned Kotzebue and not long after, this Coast Guard helicopter had arrived to pick her up.

Now the helicopter was flying low, whipping the tundra grasses flat with its huge rotor blades, scattering the caribou. And a moose. Annie wondered if it was *her* moose, but she couldn't bother to follow its flight. All she cared about was finding the talus slope where she had left Robert. Her eyes watered from the strain and her empty stomach rebelled every time the pilot circled, but she couldn't be sick, not now, when Robert was counting on her.

"Hey, take a look at that," Annie heard the copilot's voice over her headset as he pointed to something on the ground.

Robert, it just had to be Robert. But when Annie looked, there was no familiar talus slope, only open tundra. And then she saw what had attracted the copilot's attention, two men lying flat out on their stomachs, their arms thrown over their heads as if to conceal themselves. The helicopter hovered.

"How about it, Annie, do you know those men?" the pilot asked.

Annie pressed up against the window to see better. They certainly weren't anyone she knew from Little Salmon. Natives? Campers? They seemed to be dressed in some kind of camouflage outfits. Annie shook her head. "No."

"I don't like the looks of them and they've got rifles. Let's get outta here," the pilot muttered over his headset and imme-

138

diately the helicopter moved vertically straight up and Annie's stomach gave a lurch.

"Who are they?" Annie asked, closing her eyes against the nausea. Before anyone could answer, Annie suddenly guessed who they were, knew who they were.

The pilot confirmed her opinion. "Probably some kind of Soviet patrol sent out to pick you up. Did you know they were after you?"

Annie shook her head, unable to answer. A Russian patrol with guns. Even safe here in the helicopter, Annie flinched at the memory of those whistling bullets. And then she thought of Robert. That patrol might have already found their hidden mud tub, headed south toward Niyuk and come across Robert. No, Annie willed, they couldn't have.

"I'll radio in to have those two picked up," the pilot said. "They shouldn't be any problem as long as they haven't found the boy yet."

The boy. That was Robert. Annie leaned her hot forehead against the cool window and clutched her throat as if that would stop it from hurting. That was when she saw it, a blue ribbon of color in the distance that was the Lanatak River, and below, a flash of silver.

"Robert!" Annie shouted. It *was* Robert. He was on the ledge, his space blanket waving like a brave flag. The tight knot that twisted Annie's insides dissolved into warm relief as the cockpit blurred in a moment of vertigo.

It didn't take the paramedics long to strap Robert onto a stretcher and maneuver him off the ledge. When they got him back into the helicopter, Annie was waiting for him.

"Robert." It wasn't more than a whisper.

Although Robert's eyes were swollen almost shut, he turned his head at the sound of her voice. But there was no recognition. Now the door was closed and bolted and the helicopter was taking off with a roar of its engine and a piercing whine of

139

its huge blades. Without a headset to muffle the racket, Annie's head throbbed with the sound.

She leaned down and shouted. "Robert, are you all right?" Her usual dumb question. Of course he wasn't all right. All she had to do was look at him to realize that. A makeshift splint encased his leg with a wide bandage covering his forehead.

"He'll be okay after a couple of days in the Kotz hospital," one of the paramedics said as he covered Robert with a blanket and handed Annie a blanket too.

That wasn't good enough for Annie, she wanted to hear it from Robert. "Say something, Robert," she insisted. "It's me, Annie . . . Short Straw . . ."

Robert's eyes moved toward Annie, gradually focusing. "You made it, Short . . . I knew you would . . ."

"The Russian patrol. Did they find you?" Annie shouted.

Robert shook his head. "I spotted them first . . . crawled outta sight . . . they never saw me . . . what about Little Salmon?"

The pilot had already told Annie what had happened. Some natives had found the defectors' fishing boat and called the Coast Guard. As soon as the Coast Guard realized it was a Soviet boat, they had radioed Little Salmon as the nearest camp. When they couldn't raise Little Salmon, they had flown over it, spotted the wreckage and radioed for military help. It hadn't taken reinforcements long to mop up the place, take the Russians into custody and fly the Little Salmon crew back to Kotzebue.

It was hard for Annie to talk, let alone try to explain all that. "Everyone's safe," she settled for. "They're all back in Kotzebue. Dad too."

Robert smiled. It wasn't much of a smile, but it was enough, and enough too, for Annie to see that one of Robert's beautiful front teeth was chipped. He must have broken it in his fall and somehow that affected her as much as anything and she had to look away before she burst into tears. Robert didn't notice. He closed his eyes and his chest rose and fell in a steady rhythm.

Now that she knew Robert was safe, Annie could let go, too. She lay down on the stretcher next to Robert's and pulled her blanket up over her. But tired as she was, too much was going through her head for her to sleep. And then she felt Robert's fingers plucking at her clenched fist. The fingers opened her hand and clasped it. Within moments, both she and Robert were asleep.

How long Annie slept she had no idea, but vaguely she was aware that the terrible racket of the helicopter had ceased and someone was calling to her.

"Annie . . . Annie . . ."

The voice was familiar, but she couldn't place it as she struggled up through the heavy waters of her sleep.

"Annie, thank God you're all right."

It was Dad leaning over her, his face so close it was hard to focus on it. Only inches away, his half-grown beard looked prickly and his bloodshot eyes shone with tears.

They had landed. They were safe at last. "Oh, Dad . . ." It was all Annie could get out before she started crying too.

Dad leaned down and held her face gently in his hands. "Baby, baby."

"Sir, we'd like to get her in the ambulance, please." It was one of the helicopter paramedics standing behind Dad.

"Where's Robert?" The space next to Annie was vacant and she suddenly panicked. He was still out on the tundra. He was hurt and counting on her. She struggled to sit up.

"Robert's okay. He's already in the ambulance," her father reassured her. "Now let's get you settled too. Just lie down and we'll handle it."

As soon as Annie's stretcher was out of the helicopter, the

141

paramedics snapped the wheels down and pushed it across the airstrip. It had stopped raining, but the air was so heavy, Annie's face was dampened by the fine mist. Dad walked along beside her, guiding the stretcher over the bumpy spots.

Annie swallowed past her aching throat. "When did you fly out to camp, Dad?" Her sense of time was still out of sync.

"Early this morning, about seven o'clock. I picked up the camp radio here in Kotz and headed right out."

Then that must have been Dad's plane she had heard through the snow. He had been that close and yet not close at all.

"When I saw those burned-out helicopters, I couldn't imagine what had happened, though being met by Soviet submachine guns was about the last thing I expected," Dad said. "And when I realized you and Robert weren't in camp with the others, I almost went crazy."

Dad still looked haggard and when Annie glanced up at him, she realized with a start that his sideburns were flecked with gray. She didn't know if that was something new, or she just hadn't noticed before.

They were at the ambulance. The paramedics lifted Annie's stretcher through the doors, then hopped in themselves, followed by Dad. Robert, over to one side on his stretcher, raised his hand in greeting.

"Robert, good work. You saved the day, you and my Annie." Dad gave Robert a broad smile as the ambulance doors shut, the motor started up, and they were all enclosed in the anesthetic-smelling warmth.

"The Little Salmon crew's okay?" Robert's voice was a croak.

"Yeah, we've been held here in Kotz most of the day for a debriefing."

As her father spoke, for the first time, Annie registered on the time frame. "You mean everything was over before I even

142

got to Niyuk?" That couldn't be. Not after what she and Robert had been through.

Dad pressed her hand. "That doesn't negate what you did one bit, Annie. Or Robert either. You're the heroes of the hour. Of the year. Blowing up those helicopters was a real act of courage, Robert, and that was some brave move you made to kick out on your own, Annie. If I didn't know you better, I might even say it was foolhardy." Dad shook his head in mock disbelief.

Robert ran his tongue over his cracked lips. "What about the treaty?"

Dad opened Annie's hand and traced her life line across her palm. "Both governments were advised of the conspiracy and the location of the missile base, and with our approval, the Soviet government is handling it strictly as an internal matter. The treaty stands as signed."

That was close, Annie thought. Maybe coming so close would make both governments realize that the treaty had to work, that there weren't any other options.

The ambulance stopped. But as Dad stood up to help Annie, she looked him square in the face. "Wait a minute, Dad. Before we go I want to tell you something. I'm not going to college next year after graduation." Annie surprised even herself. With all the impressions and thoughts and data floating around in her head, she hadn't really counted on coming up with that.

Her father stared at her. "What do you mean?"

"I want to work at Walther Art Center instead of going to college."

Gray-green eyes impacted with identical gray-green eyes. Annie kept her gaze steady as her father glanced away first. "We'll talk about it later, Babes, when you've had some rest and feel better," he said, as if by later she would come to her senses.

143

That was all right too. Dad probably figured he could talk her out of it the way he had always been able to talk her out of anything. But this time he couldn't. Her mind was made up. If she could get through what had happened to her this past week, she could get through standing up to her father and she knew now that her decision wouldn't alienate him forever either.

As the two paramedics moved to either side of Robert's stretcher and headed him toward the door, he looked over at Annie and gave her a thumbs-up salute of encouragement.

"Wait, Robert, I forgot. I lost your good-luck cap in the river."

". . . doesn't matter . . . that cap did okay . . . by both of us . . ."

There was no denying that. "I'll see you later, Robert."

"Come on, Annie. Let's get you going too. Time's a-wastin'," Dad said.

No, it wasn't, not really. This past week was over and done with, and for that Annie was grateful, but it hadn't been wasted. Although she had been through a lot, she had come out on the other side, and with a hard-won respect for the tundra and everything that was able to survive in it. She had survived, and on the tundra's terms, too. It was something worth thinking about, but not now. For now, bed and sleep were as much as Annie could handle.